THE ALICE ENCOUNTER

THE ALICE ENCOUNTER

THE ALICE ENCOUNTER

THE ALICE ENCOUNTER

John Gribbin

Backdrop

THIS BOOK IS IN A SENSE A SEQUEL TO *DOUBLE PLANET* AND *Reunion* (two books I wrote long ago with Marcus Chown, both published by Gollancz). The events take place roughly in the 26th century—around 2550.

Two stories run in parallel:

1. Colonists on Mars, mainly the lunar "tribe", with Tugela (from the Moon colony) and Ondray (originally from Earth). This has involved abandoning the Moon as a colony, and redirecting comets to Mars to begin to thicken the atmosphere. Earth has very limited spacefaring resources, so the colonists are essentially on their own. Earth is striving to cope with climate change, with lunar experts developing plant breeding programmes (working at Moon base, to avoid gravity problem on Earth) and other techniques.

2. The close encounter / first contact mission involving the old Lagrange (L5) base adapted by an intelligent but somewhat maverick computer known as Link for starflight. The "personality" of this machine involves Ondray + Link + "Lagrange", the last of which is essentially catatonic but still provides information in response to direct questioning.

Science

THERE IS ABOUT 10 TIMES MORE DARK MATTER (DM, ALSO known here as Alice matter) than bright stuff in our Galaxy. The DM is spread out in a roughly uniform sphere (a spherical distribution of Alice stars), with our flattened disk Galaxy embedded in it. (The "Alice matter" is a kind of mirror image shadow stuff the term "looking glass matter" has been used by some scientists.) Alice matter can be turned into ordinary matter (and vice versa) by sending it through a loop of Alice string, a naturally occurring cosmic phenomenon. Aliens in the DM world, more advanced than we are, have discovered the trace of 10 per cent "normal" matter in "their" universe. And have come to investigate it. Our disk is a perturbation that they are puzzled about.

THE ALICE ENCOUNTER

THE ALICE ENCOUNTER

For Jim Lovelock, who gave us Daisyworld

Prologue

THE PEOPLE WERE AN OLD RACE, FROM A STAR SYSTEM FAR
out in the swarm surrounding the Galaxy. As individuals,
they were long-lived, and partly for this reason their evolution had been slow. But they had started on the evolutionary
path long before the Sun and its Solar System existed, and
now they were old, and wise.

Being fortunate enough to live far from the centre of the
Galaxy, their telescopes had been able to look outwards
into the Universe, to study other galaxies of stars, and to
take the temperature of the radiation that filled all of space
between the galaxies. They knew that the Universe was
expanding, and understood that this was because space
itself was stretching and expanding as time passed. They
inferred that the Universe had been born in a hot fireball,
some fourteen billion years ago—although they did not
refer to this fireball as the Big Bang, and, of course, they did
not measure time in years.

But for all their knowledge, the People still puzzled
over unsolved mysteries of the Universe. As their instruments became more sophisticated, they discovered that the
way in which distant galaxies moved could not be entirely
explained in terms of the gravitational influence of all the

visible, bright stars that they contained. There seemed to be some additional, dark matter holding the Universe together, and affecting, among other things, the way in which galaxies rotate.

The discrepancy was small—about 10 per cent. But as time passed, the observations continued to tell the same irritating story. And, besides, there were theoretical and aesthetic reasons to expect there to be about 10 per cent more matter than could be seen in the Universe, ensuring that the Universe itself could be a closed, self-contained system.

Even the Galaxy in which the People had their home was not immune from this effect. Studies of the way in which stars in the swarm were moving, under the influence of gravity, showed how much mass there must be in the Galaxy, and where it was concentrated. But counts of all the stars on the sky showed too few to provide that gravitational pull. Some of the mass seemed to be missing—or in a dark, and undetectable form.

Generations of cosmologists and philosophers argued about the implications, while the astronomers refined their observations and calculated just where this dark matter must lie. They found that it was concentrated in a thin disc, a plane almost exactly bisecting the Galaxy proper. And when, at last, spacefaring technology had developed to the point where such voyages were possible, it was natural that an expedition should be sent, diving down towards the region of gravitational anomaly within the Galaxy, in search of the missing mass.

One

THE SHIP WAS A FAT SPINDLE, ROTATING IN THE EMPTINESS OF space. It clearly was not designed to enter an atmosphere; the spindle was surrounded by intricate, inexplicable structures that seemed to have been attached almost at random. One end—one pole—was relatively free from clutter, but at the other pole three structures sprang from the surface of the spindle, like legs of a huge tripod. They met in a ball just above the pole, a ball which, although more than a hundred metres across, was dwarfed by the size of the spindle itself. Beyond the ball, a spike, long and thin, extended further unguessable hundreds of metres into emptiness. The spike was so slender that it might almost have escaped notice, should there have been any observer watching the ship from outside, except for one thing. It glowed, with a faint, blue light. The glow was associated with the stream of charged particles being forced away from the Ship, and thereby forcing the ship itself forward.

The acceleration produced was tiny, but it could be maintained for a *very* long time. And the intelligence on board the ship was patient. It had no need to worry about mundane problems like mortality, and it had expected that it could afford to take its time, sure that it would, sooner or later, come across something interesting to investigate.

Unfortunately, something interesting had turned up too soon, unexpectedly instilling an urgent need for progress through the void. But nothing could be done to increase the efficiency of the drive. In strict obedience to Newton's laws, every ion that it threw out backwards at a sizeable fraction of the speed of light gave the Ship a tiny boost forward, with action and reaction equal and opposite. The intelligence would, indeed, just have to be patient while it crawled, with exquisite slowness, outward from the orbit of Mars, towards the point of interest.

Two

ONDRAY LEANED FORWARD INTO THE WIND AS HE TRUDGED back towards the landrover. Inside the airtight suit, its flexible skin puffed out by the pressure of the air he was breathing, he could scarcely feel the thin breeze, but the sleeting dust made its direction clear, and habits of an upbringing on Earth were hard to overcome.

It was late afternoon, and the sky was streaked in spectacular hues of red; one of the first consequences of thickening the atmosphere had been to allow even more dust to stay in suspension, whipped up by the winds and falling only slowly back to the red surface of the planet. It was just something they all had to learn to live with, until a proper hydrological cycle became established to damp the desert down, and until the creeping plant cover, engineered to the best ability of the lunar farmers, had had more time to do its work.

"So far," Ondray said to himself as he reached the rover, "so good." The plantation that he had been checking on seemed to be surviving well, spreading its tendrils across the desert floor and laying down roots, locking the sands in place at the same time that it darkened the surface of the planet, decreasing the albedo of the surface and encouraging the absorption of incoming heat from the distant Sun—what little heat there was to absorb. Adapted from plants originally engineered to survive on the Moon itself, the weed needed only a trace of moisture, a little carbon dioxide, and a smidgen of nitrogen to survive. Up at the poles, specially selected lichen was darkening the surface of the white polar caps, doing the same job of darkening the surface, and hastening the meltback that was being stimulated by the increasing greenhouse effect of the thickening air.

The tracked vehicle was a cylinder, just under seven metres long and three in diameter, so that even an adult loonie could just about stand up inside. For Ondray, it was positively spacious. The main airlock was at the rear of the vehicle. He punched the entry pad, and while he waited for the lock to cycle he chinned a bar inside his helmet, causing the time to be displayed, briefly, on the inside of his visor. It was 16.19. The Martian day was 24 hours 37 minutes and something over 20 seconds long, by terrestrial timepieces, but for convenience the colony divided it up into exactly 24 Martian "hours", each subdivided into 60 Martian minutes and 3600 Martian seconds. The addition of just over one and a half terrestrial minutes to each hour wasn't enough to trouble any human biorhythms, least of all those of colonists largely brought up on the Moon, where each day/night cycle lasted a month. Their problem was getting used to the rapid succession of the days, not the slightly slower passage of the hours.

Nearly 4.20 in the afternoon. Automatically, Ondray started to look up, to the point in the northeastern sky where the former Lagrange habitat would be shining like a bright star, passing across the sky. But, of course, there was no star. Lagrange was gone, halfway to Jupiter, by now. They were on their own. So short of intelligent machinery that they had to chin bars in helmets to call up the time, and press pads on the outside of landrovers to open airlocks.

Many of the loonies still regarded even this level of technology as magic; but Ondray, brought up on the Islands, knew better. And now, Link was so far away that any messages, crawling along at the speed of light, would take more than twenty minutes to cover the gap.

Communication, of a sort, was still possible. But for the first twenty-eight years of his life, Ondray had always, except for the few days when he and Tugela had been on board the Lagrange habitat before its communications link with Earth was restored, been in instantaneous contact with the Link—his teacher, protector and best friend. Almost his symbiont. It would take more than a few months to get used to the absence. Even if the Link he had known for most of the past ten years was just a copy of the original, transferred into the memory of the Lagrange Ship, there had been no way to tell the difference.

That wasn't all that had been transferred into the memory of the Ship, but Ondray didn't want to think too deeply about the others.

He looked down again, still aware of the aching emptiness, but happy to get engrossed in routine. The lock door was open, and he stepped through, automatically punching the pad to seal it behind him. Inside, he carefully cleaned the outside of the bright yellow suit with the suction line, and cleaned all the dust he could from the floor of the lock, before removing the hard helmet from its neck ring and opening the inner door.

Tugela had left her seat at the command panel at the front of the vehicle, and was ready to take the helmet from him. She bent down, kissed him warmly.

"Welcome back."

"Hey, I've only been outside for a couple of hours."

"Two hours too long."

"You're right."

This time, he initiated the welcome home kiss. She *was* right. Any surface excursion, especially solo, was still an adventure, and merited some reward. But they were both professional enough to leave it at two kisses.

He would have liked to remove the suit completely, take a shower in the vehicle's fully equipped toilet area. But both regulations and common sense would have required him to put the suit back on afterwards, just in case; and they were only an hour's drive from the base. He could wait that long to get rid of the stickiness down his back. No point in waiting around out here.

"Everything OK?"

She nodded. "Everything OK inside."

"And outside. Let's move."

She returned to the command position, and he sat beside her. Frowning slightly, she leaned forward and touched a sequence into the panel, instructing the rover to go home. There would be no need for her to drive the vehicle manually, since it was returning along a route it knew already. But the machine was just stupid enough that it was advisable for one, or both, of them to sit up front, watching the terrain ahead through the wide windscreen.

Tired, Ondray leaned against her, swaying with the motion of the vehicle, but keeping his eyes open for trouble. Her arm came round him, automatically, and he snuggled underneath it, nestling against her slim body.

They made an odd couple—the only loonie-terrie married couple, her almost a metre taller than him—and they knew it. It was inevitable that people would smile, albeit tolerantly, at the sight of them together, and that they would keep themselves to themselves as much as possible, volunteering for field trips on which they could be alone. So they spent a lot more time together even than most married couples, and had developed an understanding that required few words between them.

"Everything OK," they both knew, was a reassuring way of describing a situation on the edge of falling apart. The Lagrange Ship should have stayed for another ten years to ensure that the colony was securely established, before setting off to explore the Galaxy. The physical link with the Earth-Moon system was broken, and could not be restored for decades, if ever. The colonists were completely on their own, dependant on their own resources, and on the supply of comets, directed by the two *Perseus* robot craft from trans-Jovian space towards Mars to build up the planet's atmosphere to a tolerable density.

Only a decade ago, it had been a *shortage* of comets that had set in train a series of events leading to the reunion between the struggling lunar colony and the surviving Earth humans on the Islands—and also to the meeting between Ondray and Tugela. Now, ironically, it was a *surplus* of comets that had caused Link to abandon them, setting off towards the outer Solar System in the Ship, and which threatened the tentative steps being made in the Islands to extend human civilization back out over the face of the Earth.

On Mars, with the 47,927 colonists protected in their five airtight domed bases, it would be almost impossible to have too many cometary impacts. But on Earth, where roughly ten times as many people lived out in the open on the Islands, the kind of environmental change that could be wrought by cometary impacts might prove devastating. And some unknown influence had disturbed—was disturbing—the cometary cloud that lay out beyond the orbit of Neptune, sending a stream of new comets falling inward, past Jupiter, past Mars, and across the orbit of the Earth itself. And sending Link, with the Lagrange Ship, out to find out why this was happening. Link had no choice. His programming required him to protect human beings, and there were a lot more human beings on Earth than on Mars.

So far, there had been no encounters. Everything *was* OK, but only just. It would take the Ship nearly two years, overall, to reach the region of disturbance in the comet cloud, even using the ion drive all the way, and taking advantage of a gravitational slingshot past Jupiter. And it would take it two years to get back, from the moment the problem was solved. Assuming it could be solved. Meanwhile, the colonists existed on a knife edge, scarcely better off than they had been back on the Moon, ten years before. But at least now their destiny lay in their own hands.

The Mars colony owed its existence to Ondray, to Tugela, and to the Link—and also to the xenophobia of all too many terries (and, it had to be admitted, not a few of the loonies as well). Genetically altered to cope with the thin atmosphere and low gravity of the Moon, back when the lunar colony had been established half a millennium ago, and further changed after the split, the loonies could never, now, adapt to life on the surface of the Earth. They could have stayed on the Moon, once contact with the Link, and through Link to the *Perseus* craft that controlled the flow of comets, carrying life-giving water and gases to renew the man-made lunar atmosphere, had been restored. But even after almost five centuries without direct contact between the two cultures, the horror of infection from the Moon was still deeply ingrained in the terrie psyche.

Not without reason. The escape of the loonie retrovirus, the DNA tripler that had provided for stability and ensured against excessive mutation in the high-rad lunar environment, had proved a disaster on Earth, locking crops, animals and people into a frozen genetic mould, with little variability and no capacity to cope with change. The thoughtless farming techniques of the twentieth and twenty-first centuries had already taken agriculture far down that path, towards huge monocultures with one species of grain covering vast tracts of land—each head of corn identical to the one next door, all superbly productive under optimum conditions, and all equally vulnerable to any change in the weather patterns or any disease that might strike.

The changes in weather patterns were the result of human activities; the new diseases came from viruses, unaffected by the DNA tripling, mutating into new forms as readily as they always had, but finding their victims no longer possessing the variety that had always, during the billions of years of natural evolution on Earth, ensured that many survived even the worst plagues. In the long run, this was as much bad news for many of the viruses as for their victims, as they ran out of victims to attack.

By the time things stabilised, only a few species had survived. As the climate settled into its new mould, forests and plains dominated by just a few species of plant, and roamed by just a few species of animal, covered much of the Earth. Human civilization survived only in the Islands, watched over by the Link, protected by a technology that was no longer understood, with the lunar adventure forgotten.

It had been Tugela's desperate flight from the Moon, seeking help to restore the flow of comets, that had restored contact, releasing the Link from the programming inhibiting it from allowing the two cultures to meet.

It had to be admitted that in some ways the reunion was timely. The slight cooling of the Sun in recent decades had begun to cause problems with the crops, and loonie skill with breeding new strains was, reluctantly, welcomed. A joint research programme, based in a sealed lunar dome and taking advantage of the high rad environment to hasten the mutation rate of plants brought up from Earth, made sense.

In return, Earth could have simply restored the flow of comets to the Moon. But how much better, in terrie eyes, to move the whole loonie problem far away, where it could not contaminate the Earth again? How much better for the loonies, surely, to have a whole planet to colonise, instead of one small Moon? A planet where gravity was only a little over twice lunar normal, about 38 per cent of Earth normal, and which already had a thin atmosphere, and water frozen beneath the surface. A planet ready to be brought to life by the skills of the loonies, and any terries crazy enough to want to join them, assisted by the leftover technology controlled by the Link, and by the judicious addition of regular comet-loads of volatiles guided into place by the *Perseus* craft.

The loonies had had little choice, but most were enthusiastic. After the chaos of the collapse of the lunar culture, a fresh start looked welcoming. At least, until it became a reality.

Three

ONDRAY TASTED THE INCOMING FLOW OF DATA FROM MARS and the Earth-Moon system. It was largely routine. Status reports on the continuing success of the plant breeding programme, and the familiar concern of the Council about changing weather patterns and the threat of wildcat comet impacts. They were a bunch of neurotics; if it had been left to the Council, Earth would never have taken action to save herself. Their reports contrasted sharply with the optimistic reports from Mars of the slow, but steady, progress with the terraforming techniques, their desire for *more* comets, not less. All equally routine stuff, and undoubtedly exaggerating the positive just as much as the terries habitually exaggerated the negative.

There was also something else from Mars, something he wasn't quite ready for yet. A personal message, full video and voice, from Ondray and Tugela. He couldn't help but be aware of it, as soon as he had tasted the incoming data bits. He knew it was no more than friendly gossip. But he had quickly shunted the data into a memory file from which it could be retrieved later.

At least there was no longer any prospect of a direct two-way conversation between the Ship and any of the planet-based fragments of humanity. He left it to the Link to compose their own routine messages, reporting all well with the Ship, the voyage and the clone body, now almost mature, in the new hibernation pod at the rear of the Ship.

That was something else Ondray would rather not think about, for now. All too soon, he knew, Link would be insisting that he carried out the final test. Nobody knew what they would find, out beyond Neptune. They might need that human body, not just in hibernation, but up and functioning independently. It might be enough to keep the Protector happy in its present state; but the present situation could not last indefinitely.

And yet, the longer Ondray remained in his present state of symbiosis with Link and the Ship, the more reluctant he was to contemplate returning to his old state. Especially in a new and untried body. Suppose something went wrong, and he got stuck in the organic state—or worse?

Four

ONDRAY RUBBED HIS WEARY EYES, BLINKED, AND TURNED away from the screen for a while to focus on something—anything—further away. The reports were only routine, just what you would expect. The Earth Council still fretting, the Link calm and reassuring. Nothing personal from his alter ego on the Ship.

Hardly worth wearing his eyes out for, but they were stuck with the primitive technology, and he had to plough through everything in case there was a nugget of valuable news or information. No Link here, any more.

In his mind's eye, his gaze stretched beyond the blank wall, out through the thin air, up across space, following the track of the communications he had just sent out in response to the latest incoming messages. First to the comsat in Mars orbit, the essential first step in their communications with both the Ship and the Earth. Then splitting off, each following their own path, one across the Solar System, almost grazing the Sun at this stage of the orbital dance of Earth and Mars, the other out, past Jupiter, aimed at a point no longer even visible.

It was different in the Islands, of course. There, they still had the old observatory and communications centre on

R'apehu, with antenna/receiver systems powerful enough to pull in the signals from beyond Jupiter, let alone those from Mars, and transmitters powerful enough to blast their messages clear across the Solar System, with no need for the stepping stone of an orbital satellite.

And they had the Link. Or *a* Link. His original Link, running the systems, providing information by voice, or by Link. Not bloody stupid screens that took ages to read and tired your eyes and brain in the reading.

The whole bloody thing was cobbled together, like that. The Mars colonists had got everything that Earth could spare, he acknowledged that. But everything that Earth could spare ran only to a few simple-minded machines. Epic work by the Ship, ferrying colonists and cargo from the Earth-Moon system to Mars under the control of the Link, had just given them a toehold on the red planet, no more. Now, the only ships they had were three Shuttles, doubtless capable of making the journey to the Earth, but each with a capacity of no more than ten people. And they had no Link at all. And yet, those hotheads in Dome Four still insisted that they wanted to go "home". Didn't they realise this *was* home, now, whatever happened? That there was no way back?

Given time, and about the same effort that had gone into the Mars colony in the first place, they could probably have built another Ship. Even a better Ship, in all except the most important detail. They couldn't replicate the Link. Link himself couldn't replicate the Link, for reasons best known to his designers.

"Programming, Ondray."

He smiled as he seemed to hear the words, Link's familiar apology for anything that had been forbidden by his designers.

"One day," he told himself. He'd broken the Link's programming before, when overriding danger had made it both necessary and possible. Maybe his counterpart was working on it, even now. "One day we'll be as clever as the Ancients. If only Tolly Hoopa and his friends would just be patient."

But even though they only had one Link, he had always been intended for a dual role—resident in the Earth systems, looking after the Islands, and also in the Lagrange systems, looking after the Moon. The only difference now was that the Lagrange systems had become the Ship, and half of the Link was now further than it had ever been from any branch of humanity, and getting further away with each passing second.

Further from anybody except the clone, that is. A copy of a Link with a copy of an Ondray and a copy of a human body. And both branches of humanity depending on the doppelgangers to solve the problem of the comets. On a Link that he could only communicate with, now, using words scrolling up a screen, and on another self who refused to communicate at all.

Five

THE DISCOVERY OF WHAT SEEMED TO BE INDIVIDUAL
shadow stars, orbiting in almost circular paths around the
centre of the galaxy and within the thin disk, came as no real
surprise to the People. If shadow matter existed, as theory
said it must, then shadow stars, and even shadow planets,
must also exist. As they got close enough to the disk for
individual stars to be resolved by their mass detectors, the
swarm on the exploration craft chose one mass anomaly,
registering as a point at this distance, and changed course
to approach it closely.

It was also no real surprise that, as they approached
the shadow star more closely, slowing as they did so, with
detectors at maximum sensitivity to ensure that they missed
nothing interesting in this region of the shadow world, those
detectors began to find traces of other objects, undoubtedly
planets, orbiting the shadow star. At least four large planets
were distinguishable in the gravitational signature of the
system, with other traces indicating three or more smaller
objects closer in to the star, where they were hard to distin-
guish from the gravitational noise of the star itself.

The initial plan was for the swarm to place their craft in
orbit around the outermost planet, using one probe to take

samples from it while the second probe was sent inward to study the star itself. Caution and patience were the characteristics that had enabled the People to survive and spread through such a large volume of space; the swarm were too cautious to risk taking their own craft into the gravitational anomaly marking the shadow star itself, and amply patient enough to wait for an automated probe to take what risks there were and to report back to them.

But the meticulous plans had been thrown into confusion by an unexpected discovery. Before they had reached the orbit of the outermost planet, their slowing craft had suddenly been surrounded by thousands—millions—of tiny gravitational anomalies. They seemed to be moving through a belt of debris, orbiting the parent star—if, indeed, that anomaly was a star in the shadow world—at greater distances than any large planet. Nothing like it was known in all the star systems explored by the People in the real world. And since the objective of their expedition was to explore the unknown, this was clearly the place to start. The planets could wait—although there seemed no reason not to send the second probe on its inward trajectory towards the supposed shadow star.

Even at their now leisurely pace, it required a major course correction to bring their craft into a circular orbit moving with the belt of debris. But their gravitational drive, gripping the very fabric of spacetime itself, was amply adequate to the task.

The ripples from the manoeuver spread out from the craft like ripples from a stone tossed into a pond, shaking the nearby masses and flinging many of them into new orbits, some diving inward, past Neptune, towards the Sun, while others were shaken loose from the Solar System entirely and escaped into the depths of interstellar space. Several hundred of the cometary nuclei were affected, one way or the other;

but this was only a tiny fraction of the total number in the belt, and left plenty more for the swarm to study.

Six

Tarragon didn't waste any time on courtesies. He came straight in to Ondray's office, flung himself in the chair, and spoke.

"We've got more trouble out at Terranova."

Tarragon owed his position as Ondray's number two—strictly speaking, number two to the Ondray-Tugela duopoly, but many of the loonies were still reluctant to accept a female leader—to his unique background. Once a trainee for the Priesthood on the Moon, he had seen the light and quit, becoming a leading member of the resistance movement in the City in the last days. He knew the ways of the one-time City folk, both the diehards who still tried to cling to remnants of the old religion and the younger element eager to make a go of the colonization of Mars. He'd seemed ideal to be the top man in the main settlement, the three linked domes of New Tycho, where most of the City dwellers from the Moon had been settled. If there was going to be any unrest, it had seemed that this was where it would be, and that Tarragon was the man to stamp it out. Which automatically made him Ondray's number two.

But they had been wrong—or, maybe, Tarragon was so good at his job that what was going on out at Terranova simply looked bad by comparison.

Almost five hundred kilometers away from New Tycho, most of the former farmers from the Moon were housed in the other two domes, Four and Five, which together made up the Terranova settlement. The location of the two settlements had been difficult to decide. Far enough apart so that if a disaster—like an unscheduled comet impact—struck one, the other would survive. Close enough to offer each other help and assistance in any lesser emergency. In theory, either colony could survive on its own, now. In practice, any sensible colonization plan would have included at least three settlements each the size of the triple-domed New Tycho. The existing colonies operated on a knife edge, and everybody knew it.

But the knowledge affected different people in different, and not always easily predictable, ways. The trouble had come not from the timorous City folk, but from the hardy farmers, who Ondray, and Link, had expected to be better able to cope with the conditions.

In many ways, after all, those conditions were better than they had been in the last days on the Moon. More air, crops that were beginning to spread, if not actually to thrive, and, by no means least, no open warfare with the City.

But for now the colonists were still largely restricted to the domes, until the oxygen content of the air built up. That had come much harder for the farmers than for the City dwellers, to whom New Tycho was not so different to their old, familiar surroundings. The trouble here was getting enough of them to spend long enough outside to get the work done. But at least the former City folk were used to being told what to do—which, 20:20 hindsight gleefully reminded Ondray, the farmers most definitely were not used to. Independence was their watchword. Which led to endless trouble; what was it *this* time?

"Tolly Hoopa?"

"And the rest of Dome Four. A petition, now. A formal request that we recall the Ship and take them all back to the Moon. Redirect the flow of comets, now that both *Perseus* craft are operational, to the Moon as well as to Mars. And there's a subtle bit about the value of having a third branch of civilization on the Moon, as backup to Earth and ourselves."

"Why can't Mandelbrot keep them under control?"

"He's older than Tolly's crowd. Tired. Don't forget, he was really only a war leader, elected for the duration. He never anticipated spending years helping to organise the Great Trek across space, then trying to keep the squabbling elements happy stuck inside a couple of lousy domes."

"He's kept Dome Five happy."

"Largely by keeping the oldsters together in there. If he'd spread the groups more evenly between the two domes, Terranova might be in a happier state now."

"And if I'd spread people more evenly between Terranova and New Tycho, we might not have any problem of this kind."

"Or we might have farmers and City folk fighting in the corridors in all five domes. You did the best you could, Ondray. And the Link agreed."

"Yeah." The Link. Always the bloody Link. "He" would have a solution to the present problem, no doubt. Hell, if it came to it Link *could* take the rebels back to the Moon. If only he didn't have more pressing problems to attend to. If only the laws of orbital mechanics weren't so unforgiving.

"Don't they understand you can't just call the Ship back?"

"I've told them, Ondray. Just as you have. Just as Link did, before he left. I don't know if they are really that stupid, or just playing ignorant. But they seem to think you can turn a Ship around as easily as a horse—or a landrover."

"I'll have to talk to Tolly myself. In the flesh."

Tarragon leaned forward in his chair, grinning.

"I hoped you'd say that. I can look after things here while you're gone."

"It'll only be about five days, at most."

The grin faded. Tarragon looked down at the floor, then back up into Ondray's eyes.

"Uh, Ondray. One word of advice."

Ondray waited.

"It might be best if you didn't take Tugela along with you."

Ondray swung round in his seat, facing his screen, sideways on to Tarragon.

"For comet's sake, Tarragon. There's nothing in this. Tolly used to have a crush on her, that's all. From the last days on the Moon, when he was just a kid. She was a heroine to all of them, then, and he was just enough younger than her to have been more struck by hero worship than most."

"It really is more than that, Ondray. He tries to keep it under control, I'll give him that. And I know it's entirely one-sided. But he's bitterly jealous. Go on your own, and he'll be reasonable, by his lights. But take her along and he might get irrational—"he raised a hand to stop the protestations Ondray was about to make. "Not that way. Not to interfere with her. But it might focus his dislike of terries into something more personal. Make it impossible for you to get him to see reason about staying here. You understand?"

"I understand what you are saying, Tarragon. I don't agree, but I understand. And just in case you're right, I'll follow your advice. It'll only be for a few days, and there's plenty for Tugela to do here."

Seven

ONE WATCHER CONTINUED TO WORRY ABOUT THE CHANGES. From the ground, limited to the one observing site on the mountaintop of R'apehu, it had been difficulty, at first, to be sure what was happening. But when satellite mounted instruments had become available again after the reunion, only a few years' data had been needed to confirm the trend. The Sun was getting cooler.

The effect was still small, barely three per cent, overall. It seemed to be linked with a build-up in sunspot activity, with increasing numbers of dark spots spreading over the face of the Sun in each 11-year cycle, that had been the first clue to some changes in the pattern that had held stable for centuries.

The watcher was puzzled by details of the change. Old records, preserved in memory since before the watcher became self aware, said that such changes had happened in the past, but that when the Sun cooled sunspot activity declined. And the increased spottiness of the Sun did not follow the usual pattern, building up at high solar latitudes early in the cycle and drifting towards the solar equator as the cycle progressed. Instead, there seemed to be a new concentration of spots at low latitudes at all times, in addition to the usual pattern.

But the astronomical subtleties were not important. The cooling was. On Earth, the modest cooling need not be a problem, provided it did not continue for much longer. The new crops showed promise, and, besides the Islands were still thinly populated. If solar cooling was all they had to worry about and the worst came to the worst, some of the land in the south could be abandoned, temporarily, until this solar hiccup reversed itself.

But the watcher worried about the Mars colony, now without their own Link, trying to swim against the tide and warm the planet in the face of a solar cooling. Much more of this, and in spite of their efforts to strengthen the Martian greenhouse effect the Sun would be cooling the planet faster than they could warm it. And yet, the balance of potentials was clear. The comet problem *had* to take precedence. It affected more people, and it posed the threat of major catastrophe, not a slow decline. It was right that the Ship should have left the Martian colony to fend for itself for a time. It was right, but it didn't make the watcher feel any happier about the situation.

The watcher pondered on these points as it tasted the flow of messages. All the traffic between Earth and Mars, of course, passed through the comcentre/observatory on R'apehu. And all traffic between Mars and the Ship also passed that way, taking advantage of the powerful receiver/antenna systems. *This* Link really did live up to its name. Which meant that it was the most well-informed intelligence in the Solar System—at least, as far as human activities were concerned.

Eight

IT WAS AGAINST ALL THE RULES TO GO ALONE, BUT WITH Link gone there was nobody here to overrule Ondray's decision. If he couldn't take Tugela with him, then, he'd told Tarragon, to hell with it; he wouldn't take anyone. Tarragon had remained silent. If anyone else had tried it, Ondray himself would have overruled them. But there was nobody to overrule him—except Tugela, and she understood him, and the reason why she had to stay behind, well enough not to make more than a token effort to dissuade him.

There was no real danger. The landrover might be stupid, but it knew the way to Terranova all right. It just needed a little human guidance where there might have been minor recent changes in the landscape caused by the increasingly strong winds—winds that were welcome as a sign that their efforts at improving the climate on Mars were beginning to work, but were a minor inconvenience at present. Maybe more than a minor inconvenience—it was the winds that were helping to keep the farmers cooped up in the domes for so much of the time, giving them time to think, and giving Tolly Hoopa an opportunity to foment dissent.

With a full crew of three, two on duty and one resting in one of the bunks at the rear of the vehicle's cabin, it was a

36-hour run from New Tycho to Terranova, nonstop. But hardly anyone bothered to keep going through the night anyway, and Ondray would be quite happy to make half the journey then take a break, getting a quiet night's sleep and a chance to think out his course of action. He was missing Tugela, already; he'd miss her more, tonight. But at least nobody else could get to him with demands for help to solve some stupid problem that should never have arisen in the first place.

His inner anger and tension began to dissolve as he sat in the left-hand seat at the front of the cockpit, watching the landscape roll by, his conscious mind almost blank while he let the subconscious worry away at the problem. By the time he'd slept on it, he expected to have a better idea of what to do, even if he hadn't devoted too much conscious effort to it. It was the way he always worked best—get away on his own, relax, and as if by magic new ideas and answers to old puzzles would pop into his head. He'd used to wonder if it might not, somehow, be Link's doing. But now he was on his own, as never before, and his ability to think seemed to be standing up pretty well under the strain.

The kilometers rolled slowly by as he watched the changing, but always similar, landscape. The route meandered between columns of rock, carved by eons of dry, windblown dust, and across—sometimes along—what could only be dried out river beds. Gullies criss-crossed the barren landscape. It looked for all the world as if it were the aftermath of a great flood, as if the water might come roaring along the river beds, splashing down the gullies, at any moment. But Link had told them that there had been no running water on Mars for hundreds of millions of years.

There was frozen water, below the surface, where it had stayed for all that time. And there was even surface water, in the polar caps, mixed with the frozen carbon dioxide that was their main constituent. There was even water vapour in the air, tiny traces that sublimated from the respective polar caps each spring, changing straight from the solid state to the vapour without bothering to pass through the liquid phase in between, and changing back to ice as winter set in. But there was still no liquid water on Mars, except for the stuff within the domes, and in the tanks of the landrovers like the one in which he was riding.

Unaware, consciously, of the direction in which his subconscious mind had been wandering, Ondray decided that it would do no harm to check the contents of the water tanks. Of course, there was plenty. More than enough for a crew of three to complete the journey from New Tycho to Terranova and back without being replenished; at least three times as much as he could possibly need. The same applied to the other essentials—food, and oxygen. Oxygen was most important of all, and, inevitably, set the upper limit on how long he could stay in the landrover. But even there, there was enough for one man for over 200 hours.

So, as he'd told Tugela, he was actually safer, in some ways, on his own. His air would last longer, in any minor emergency. And in any major emergency—like an unscheduled comet impact alongside the rover—that wrecked the vehicle's life support systems, he'd be just as dead with two companions as he would on his own.

But the chance of such a catastrophe was remote. There were no incoming comets within a week of Mars at present, although there were two rogues crossing the orbit of Mars, far to one side, and heading uncomfortably close to Earth; and the landscape had scarcely changed in millions of years. What could go wrong? Even if he brought Tolly Hoopa straight back with him, without waiting to replenish, there'd be ample supplies of air, and everything else, for the two of them on the return journey.

Now, where had *that* thought come from?

He stopped checking the supplies, and leaned back in his seat to worry his way back along the thread of logic that his brain had been putting together without his knowledge. He hadn't even slept on it, yet, and already the subconscious was at work. So, who needed the Link?

It made sense. Mandelbrot was still respected by most of the farmers. Tolly was the leader of the opposition to Mandelbrot at Terranova, as well as being the originator of this ridiculous idea that the Ship could be called back to return half the Terranovans to the Moon. If Tolly wouldn't see reason, bring him back to New Tycho—*straight* back, before any of the hotheads who followed him could do anything foolish—for more lengthy discussions.

Ondray grinned to himself. *Very* lengthy discussions. Let the rebellion, such as it was, die out for lack of a leader, through sheer boredom. After all, time was on his side. The longer he could delay things, the more obvious it would become that the changes they were wreaking on this planet were becoming effective. Get those farmers out on the land, where they belonged, and they'd be too damned tired to think about rebellion, apart from anything else.

Climate changes. He leaned forward again, gazing up through the bubble of clear plastic at the clouds. The sky was still red, the air carrying a burden of dust which reduced visibility and kept the landrover's speed down to this tedious crawl. But now there were real clouds up there, clouds containing water vapour, as well.

He knew they were there. Ground-based instruments, peering upward through the murk, said they were; and the instruments on board the satellite that Link had left to watch over them, combining the duties of weather watcher and communications link, with Earth and on to the Ship itself, were even now looking down on the clouds from above, studying them spectroscopically and monitoring the build-up of water content from day to day.

"Just give me some rain," Ondray thought. "That'll take the wind out of Tolly Hoopa's sails."

Nine

DATA FLOWING BACK FROM THE PROBE SHOWED THAT THE anomaly really was a shadow star. The probe settled into a preliminary investigative orbit, about ten per cent of the radius of the object inside the outer boundary of the star. Its gravitational sensors probed inward, investigating the mass distribution within the object, and found a dense core, extending over no more than a quarter of the distance from the centre to where the probe now orbited. This was clearly the source of energy, very similar to the structure of stars in the real universe. There had to be a central source of energy, of course, to prevent gravity from squeezing such a large concentration of matter down into a ball no bigger than one of the small planets orbiting the shadow star.

The sensors showed that this core contained almost half of the total mass of the anomaly, compressed into one sixty-fourth of its volume, and the swarm had no intention of risking the probe in such a dense concentration of shadow matter until they were satisfied that there was, in fact, no risk at all.

Even in the more tenuous outer layer of the shadow star, where the probe now orbited, the temperature must be at least as great as the temperature at the surface of a star in the real universe. The atmosphere would be a seething mass of convective activity, which would buffet any shadow-ship that could withstand the intense heat. And there must be billions of shadow particles, radiation from the nuclear processes that kept the shadow star hot, zipping through the probe every second.

But none of this was directly apparent to the probe or its instruments. It could almost have been orbiting a black hole, for all the physical effect the shadow star had on it.

There was one difference. Moving parallel to the probe, but at a safe distance from it, the loop, guided by the gravitational fingers of the probe's spacewarp facility, swept through the convective zone of the shadow star, leaving a streamer of star stuff behind it in the real world. Unlike the probe, or the parent craft of the swarm, the loop existed in *both* worlds at once—and any material passing through the loop was twisted out of its original universe and into the other one.

The streamer of stuff trailing out behind the loop was reminiscent of the tail of a comet, but much hotter. Cooling rapidly in the empty space of the real universe, it radiated across the electromagnetic spectrum as nuclei and electrons, converted into their counterparts in the universe occupied by the People, recombined to form stable atoms in a coiling, dissipating cloud.

The spectroscopic data showed that the material was remarkably similar to ordinary star stuff, but that there were intriguing differences, subtleties that would require long and painstaking observations to unravel. Physical samples would be taken from the cloud later, once the remote analysis had revealed all it could.

Data flowed steadily out from the probe, at the speed of light, to the parent craft. It was clear to the swarm that there was no risk, in the present situation, and that ample time could be taken for the required analysis. They were also preoccupied with investigating the strange ring of material they had discovered in the outer reaches of this shadow system. They were in no hurry.

Had the swarm thought to consider the possibility, they might well have realised the implications of their probe's activities for the shadow star itself. With hot material being stripped away from within the convective zone in the outer layers of the star, it was inevitable that the layer would cool slightly, suppressing convection in the region being swept through by the loop. The effect was small, but significant. Heat lost through the loop into the real world could not, of course, be available to radiate outward from the surface of the star in the shadow world, and it would cool slightly.

Although there was no way for the swarm to know this, the collapse of the convective zone resulting from the cooling would also disturb the magnetic field of the star in the region near the probe. In the convective zone, electrons were stripped from nuclei to form a hot plasma, a sea of charged particles. Electrically charged particles, tangled with the star's magnetic field, would drag field lines down with them as convection subsided, producing loops and knots stretching up to the surface itself, where the magnetic disturbances would feed back upon the charged particles at the surface, triggering the production of a rash of dark spots on the face of the star.

The loss of mass, and any side effects, would, however—as the swarm appreciated—have no significance in the long run. Analysis of the gravitational data showed that the shadow star contained about a thousand times as much mass as even the largest of its attendant planets. If the energy generation process were as efficient in the shadow world as in the real world (which, admittedly, had yet to be proved) it would have converted no more than the equivalent of one third of the mass of that planet into energy during its lifetime; it could amply afford to lose about the same amount of mass through the loop in the course of the probe's investigations. After the probe had finished, things would quickly settle back down to normal in the shadow world.

Ten

THE FIRST DAY'S JOURNEY HAD BEEN UNEVENTFUL, BUT NOT
quite routine. There was enough novelty in the build-up
of cloud to encourage Ondray to maintain a lively interest
in his surroundings, pondering the implications of what he
could see. It was strange to think that within a generation or
two the red dust outside might be covered by the creeping
vegetation and low shrubs that seemed to be surviving
effectively on the test plots; strange to think that with dust
washed from the air by rain, and molecules of water vapour
present in profusion to scatter the shorter wavelengths
of sunlight, the sky itself would be blue, if always a paler
shade of blue than the skies of Earth. How much of it, he
wondered, would he live to see with his own eyes?

The mixture of nostalgia for his past life on Earth, and
vicarious anticipation of the future he would never see on
Mars, remained with him as he parked the vehicle carefully
alongside a low mound, in the lee from the prevailing wind,
where tendrils of dust, whipped off the top of the mound,
streamed over the bubble of the cockpit, rather than threatening to build up around the balloon tyres of the landrover.
Not that the amount of dust that could build up in one night
would be any handicap to the large wheels in the morning,

but security had become ingrained in Ondray over the past few years.

Or perhaps his subconscious was at work again, encouraging him to be ultra-cautious in choosing his parking spot for the night, in some sort of compensation for the slightly less cautious, and strictly forbidden, activity which the subconscious knew he had planned, even before the conscious part of his brain acknowledged it to itself.

The idea surfaced into his conscious while he was talking to Tugela over the comlink. He'd already checked with Tarragon that everything was OK at New Tycho, and the automated systems had logged his position to the nearest centimetre or so with the aid of the satellite. There was nothing new from Terranova, where Tolly Hoopa had agreed to wait for Ondray to discuss the situation with him before pressing for any immediate action. The conversation with Tugela was more personal. He told her how much he missed her, that he wished she could be out here with him, to see firsthand the changes that were beginning to take place in the Martian atmosphere.

"We can see the clouds from here. The satellite data suggest there could be precipitation within the next 48 hours."

"Rain?"

"More likely snow. A light dusting of snow."

"Well, that should be enough to make those farmers see sense. Looks like I'll only have to stall Tolly for a few days."

There was a silence, stretching for what seemed like minutes, but could only have been a few seconds. He resisted the impulse to reach out and touch her image on the screen. It was then that the idea surfaced from his subconscious.

"I'm going out to take a look."

Her image leaned forward.

"No! Not on your own."

"It's safe enough. Besides, I need some fresh air."

She frowned, ignoring the joke, then smiled. An artificial smile; her eyes were still worried. But he appreciated it.

"Don't be long, then."

"No. A few minutes, that's all. I want to watch the sunset."

"Better leave you to it, then. Less than half an hour to go."

"Yeah."

"I'll be watching it, too."

"Yeah."

She understood. They might be tens of kilometers apart, but they could still stand on the desert together, watching the same sunset.

"Ondray . . ." her voice tailed off.

"Yeah?"

She shook her head. "Doesn't matter. It'll keep until you come back. Take care, now."

"Yeah. Take care yourself."

And she broke the connection.

Struggling into the bright yellow suit, he wondered what she had been about to tell him. Were there problems back at New Tycho that he wasn't officially supposed to know about? Or was it something personal? Something about Tolly Hoopa, maybe?

He shrugged mentally. No use worrying. She'd tell him when she was good and ready.

With the suit on, helmet in place, he stepped into the airlock, and waited for it to complete its cycle. Outside, the setting Sun was casting long shadows from the humps and ridges, making strange, dark shapes on the desert floor. The wind had dropped with the Sun, and enough dust had dropped as well to leave reasonably clear visibility. The sky was spectacularly streaked with red, shading to pink clouds overhead, and to a deep, dark black, in which the first stars were starting to appear, on the opposite horizon. He really didn't have long, and he didn't intend to do anything *really* foolish, like staying out after dark.

In the low gravity, it was easy to climb to the top of the mound, even with muscles that had become acclimatised to Mars. He would have a terrible time adapting back if he ever went back to Earth, he thought. Not that there was much chance of that. He wouldn't live anywhere without Tugela, and if there was one place she certainly couldn't live it was on the surface of the Earth.

He stood for a moment, watching the stretching shadows, the deepening red of the setting Sun. Thinking of Tugela, out in front of Dome One, watching the same scene. It *had* to be worthwhile. All the sacrifices, all the risks, even the problems with the farmers. A whole new world was at stake. It *had* to work out, surely?

It was darker than he had intended before Ondray left the top of the mound, but his helmet light provided ample illumination for the short downhill stroll back to the landrover, a brightly lit landmark only a few tens of metres away. It was back on level ground, in the lee of the mound, that he saw the glitter.

He stopped. There was a small hollow there, well shielded by the rocky outcrop. Something in the hollow was reflecting the light from his lamp.

He crouched down, tilting his head forward to direct the full glare of the lamp into the hollow. Reached out with one finger to touch the bright surface of the rock.

His glove left a dark streak on the white, reflecting surface.

Ice.

Frost.

Tiny crystals of ice, sublimating out of the air onto the cold rock. Not that unexpected, really, as the moisture content of the air increased. But a welcome sight, nonetheless.

He started to stand up. But there was something else. Finding it difficult to believe what he was seeing, Ondray knelt down on the surface, ignoring the faint risk of a sharp piece of rock puncturing his suit, and brushed gently at the dust with the gloved fingers of both hands.

In the hollow, directly below the frost covered rock surface, partly buried in the drifting dust, there was a plant. It was a creeper, the same as the ones on the test plots at New Tycho, firmly rooted, already sending its tiny tendrils out across the dust, seeking convenient spots in which to put down more roots, developing a spreading mat of vegetation across the desert, locking the shifting dust in place.

Ondray sat back on his heels, stunned. He could hardly have asked for a clearer sign that the colony was on the right track. He'd bring Tolly here, tomorrow, to this very spot, to see for himself. Surely *that* would dampen his enthusiasm to abandon everything, and go back to the Moon?

He tried to think through the logic of how the plant could have got here. It was too far, surely, for any wind-blown seeds to have carried? And the plants back at New Tycho weren't setting seed yet, anyway.

But it was right next to the beaten track between New Tycho and Terranova, which was why he was here. Could it be chance—some seed carried here from the plantations on the tread of a tyre, or the foot of a pressure suit? Or maybe one of the team from New Tycho, doing a quiet bit of private agricultural work, scattering a few seeds around when they had stopped for an overnight break on a previous journey between the two colonies.

Either way, the plant shouldn't have survived. Even the hardy vegetation, tailored to cope with the Martian conditions, still needed careful tending in the test plots, until the climate improved another notch or two. It was just luck that this one seed had found itself in the frost hollow in the lee of the mound, protected from the scouring winds, and provided with occasional traces of moisture as the increasing water content of the atmosphere encouraged the formation of night frosts.

Luck, but also a clear sign of the adaptability and toughness of life.

For the first time, Ondray realised that whatever happened to the human colonies, the face of the planet had been changed for good. If they could all go back to the Moon tomorrow, or if they were all wiped out by a succession of comet impacts, life would still be here, in the form of these plants. Many might die, no longer tended by human horticuluralists; but some would survive, and spread. The more they spread, the more the surface would change, absorbing more solar heat. At the same time, the lichens at the poles would be doing their work. In a hundred, or a thousand, years from now, with or without more human help, Mars would be transformed.

He made his way back to the landrover, and pondered over the implications while he went through the ritual of vacuuming off the dust and de-suiting. It was spectacularly good news, surely enough to shake the farmers into seeing sense. There might be more plants, out there, in other little pockets. But he wanted to take things slowly. Bring Tolly back, and let him be as surprised by the discovery as Ondray had been. Then, together they could make the announcement, from New Tycho. Send out a team to look for more plants, and to seed other promising pockets. Try to find out who was responsible for this unofficial plantation—he was increasingly sure that the plant had not got there by accident—and put them in charge.

Such isolated plots couldn't contribute much to changing the planet, but every little helped. And think of the psychological boost if there were plants dotted about along the route from New Tycho to Terranova, visible even from the cockpits of the landrovers! There'd be no shortage of volunteer drivers for the run, when they had real vegetation to monitor by the roadside.

Tired, but contentedly wrapped in the secret he intended to hug to himself for another couple of days, Ondray checked over the vehicle, shut down everything except the life support systems and a dim red cabin light, and settled into his bunk for a more relaxing sleep than he had anticipated at the outset of the journey.

Eleven

THE SHIP HAD PASSED TURNOVER, CROSSING THE ORBIT OF
Saturn backwards, with its drive now working just as hard
to slow it as it had been, for the first part of the voyage, to
increase its speed. Of course, Saturn was nowhere to be
seen. Far away on the other side of its orbit, its tiny image
would have been lost in the glare from the Sun itself, if
Ondray had bothered to direct the telescope that way. By
taking advantage of the great mass of Jupiter to provide a
gravitational slingshot effect, stealing momentum from the
giant planet and speeding up the Ship while slowing Jupiter
itself by a minute amount in its orbit, thereby satisfying the
unbreakable law of conservation of momentum, they had
had no alternative but to choose a trajectory which gave a
wide berth to Saturn.

It was, after all, only on very rare occasions that the
changing alignments of the outer planets, each travelling
at its own speed in its own orbit, would make it possible
for a single spacecraft to choose an outward trajectory
that would fly by more than one of them. On this occasion, the planets could wait; all of Link's skill had gone
into choosing a gravity-assist trajectory that would leave
them on course for a rendezvous with the anomaly out

there beyond Neptune, the source of the disturbance in the cometary belt.

And, with the voyage more than half over, Ondray could no longer find any excuse to justify, even to himself, further delays in testing the clone body.

He could see the body, lying in the opened hibernation pod, ready for him. A few wires and two thin tubes were still connected, but they could quickly be removed by the spider-like robots if he decided to go ahead. *When* he decided to go ahead. He could taste the flow of data from the routines that monitored the state of the clone. Everything normal. Pulse and breathing were there, but slow, corresponding to a state between full hibernation and consciousness. All of the attendant robots were sitting quietly beside the pod, spider-like legs folded under them, with nothing more to do until he made the next move.

Still he procrastinated. Did he really look like that? He supposed his old body must have been just like this—except that his old body carried a scar on the palm of its left hand, plus various other traces of the rough and tumble of organic life, and had a physiological age of 28 Earth years, now. While this copy had a skin as smooth and perfect as that of a new born baby, and, even though its development had been accelerated in the tank during the voyage, a physiological "age" corresponding to early maturity—perhaps 20 Earth years.

The contemplation wasted several hundred microseconds.

He quickly tasted the background flow of data concerning the running of the Ship. Another thousand or so microseconds. Everything was normal. No excuse for further delay.

He remembered, when he was a small child, going swimming in the lake, high in the hills behind his home. The moment of delicious anticipation, half excitement, half fear, standing in the cool morning air, waiting to make the first plunge into the still, cold waters.

"Better in than out, Link."

"You're ready?"

"As ready as I'll ever be. Make the transfer."

He was asleep, dozing in a comfortable bed, just emerging from the *strangest* dream.

"Ondray?"

"Link?"

He opened his eyes, blinking up at the featureless ceiling. His pulse hammered in his ears; he was uncomfortably aware of the background noise of his body, the whisper of air flowing in and out of his lungs, the creak of muscle and bone as he moved. But he felt small, isolated. Something was missing.

"Not a dream, then."

"No, Ondray, not a dream. How are you?"

He remembered everything. Remembered the Link, his own life as part of the Ship; remembered the implanted communications web that would maintain his contact with the Link while he was in the organic body.

It worked! And he wasn't entirely alone, even here!

At least, he *supposed* that it had worked, that he remembered everything. How would he know, after all, if he had forgotten something?

Ondray pushed the thought firmly to the back of his mind. He sat up, grabbing at the side of the pod for support as a wave of dizziness swept over him. His hand, rubbing against the side of the pod, gripping it harder than he had intended, hurt. His back was sore, where it had been lying in one position for too long. And the nose of this body needed blowing. "Comets," he thought, "if this is organic life, forget it."

The sooner he completed those tests, the sooner he could download back into the Ship's systems. Then, with any luck, he'd never have to use the body again—it was, after all, only for emergencies, and to keep the Protector, what was left of him, happy.

"OK, Link. Get me some clothes. And let's see if this body really does qualify as a human being."

Twelve

THE TWIN DOMES OF TERRANOVA ROSE QUICKLY OVER THE
horizon as Ondray kept the rover bouncing along the track
at its fastest safe speed. It still surprised him how quickly
the vehicle could complete the journey once its destination
was in sight; the closeness of the horizon was something
that his Earth-trained senses would never get used to. But
why worry? It seemed to make the journey—*any* journey—
shorter than it really was.

The domes were each identical to the three domes of
home, back at New Tycho. There should have been three
domes here, of course, providing multiple redundancies in
case of any problems. But there had been a limit to how
much could be done with the resources cannibalised from
the Moon, and no hope of lifting significant amounts of
material out of the gravity well of Earth, even if the terries
would have considered offering that kind of help.

At least the shuttle was parked at a safe distance, away
from the domes, noticeable only because of the way it caught
the light of the Sun. Like the shuttle at New Tycho, and the
third one safe in orbit, ready to be called down if required,
it was more a symbol than anything else, a reminder that
they were not completely cut off from the Earth-Moon

system, even though the Ship had gone. The sight of the shuttles, parked out on the dusty plains near the two colonies, provided, he knew, an important psychological link with what some of the colonists still regarded as home.

They were of little practical use, with their carrying capacity so limited. But they stood as a symbol that the Mars colonists were part of a space-faring community spread across the inner Solar System, not an abandoned outpost.

For himself, he would rather they were all in orbit, and that everyone here regarded Mars as home. That they all faced up to the fact that they *were* an abandoned outpost, and would stand or fall by their own efforts. But all in good time. As Link had taught him, it was often best to make haste slowly.

He drove straight in to the big airlock, which had opened at his approach. It closed behind him as he halted the vehicle, leaving it in the centre of the garage. No point in parking it properly over by the service area; he was here on a flying visit only. There would be no point in unsuiting once he got inside, either. He had showered, and was clean and fresh, and wouldn't need to use the toilet facilities here in the next hour or so. The suit itself was hardly necessary, but regulations—regulations that he had helped to draft—insisted that it had to be worn even for the short walk across the garage to the human-sized (loonie human-sized) inner airlock that gave access to the base. After all, there was only one door between the garage area and the outside world. And although he knew that this particular rule was as often honoured in the breaking as in the obedience, as co-leader of the colony he could hardly be seen to be breaking it himself. So he was fully suited, but with his helmet under his left arm, as he stood in the inner lock, waiting for it to complete its cycle.

As the door slid open, he saw two figures waiting to greet him. Mandlebrot, the aging leader of the farmers, who had played a key role in their rebellion on the Moon, all those years ago. And Kirt Hoffa, the young administrator—another of those re-treaded trainee priests. You had to say one thing for the priesthood—they trained good administrators.

He shook hands with both of them.

"Where's Hoopa?"

"In my office," Hoffa replied. "It's on this corridor. You can de-suit, smarten up and still be there in ten minutes."

Ondray shook his head. "I don't want to waste time. Take me straight there. And send someone to get a suit for Hoopa."

"Uh, he seems to have anticipated you, Ondray. He's fully suited already."

Ondray smiled, thinly. Tolly Hoopa was no fool, all right. He knew that he was the focal point for this nonsense, and he knew what he would do if he were in Ondray's shoes. Which suggested to Ondray that he was working along the right lines.

He spoke to Mandelbrot as they followed Hoffa along the gently curving corridor.

"No change in the situation here?"

Mandelbrot looked tired, older even than his years. He surely couldn't be much over fifty, Earth chronology. But he seemed ready to give up. His voice was low, dispirited, as he replied.

"No change. They demand the recall of the Ship, to take everyone who wants to go back to the Moon."

"How many?"

"Less than a hundred activists. Perhaps ten times as many sympathisers."

"Less than five per cent of the population of Terranova."

"But half the people here would go back to Luna if they had the choice."

And one of them, Ondray realised for the first time, was Mandelbrot himself. He'd simply seen too many changes in his life. No wonder this petty rebellion hadn't been nipped in the bud long since.

It was his mistake, of course. Mandelbdrot was the wrong man for the job. But at least things hadn't got completely out of hand. He could sort out this problem with Tolly Hoopa, find someone else to take over from Mandelbrot, who had earned a graceful retirement by any standards, and get things back on the road. What with the feeling of relief that things weren't as black as the messages from Terranova had been painting them, and the still suppressed delight of his discovery the night before, Ondray was happier than he had been in weeks as they reached the entrance to Kirt Hoffa's office.

They stopped.

"I'll go in alone," he said. "Tell traffic we're leaving in half an hour. No need to service the rover—I've still got more than enough of everything to get to New Tycho, and back again if I wanted to."

They nodded, and turned away. The stoop in Mandelbrot's shoulders was even more pronounced. *He knows*, thought Ondray. *He knows he's let me down, and he knows that I know he knows.* For a moment, he wanted to run after the old hero, tell him everything was all right. But he suppressed the urge. Everything was *not* all right, yet, even though it could have been worse. He hadn't asked to be co-leader of these colonies, but if they wanted him in the job he'd do it, as best he could. Even if that meant leaving an old hero uncomforted.

He turned and opened the door. Tolly Hoopa had been sitting on the edge of the table inside, but he stood as Ondray entered, towering over the smaller figure of the terrie. He wore a bright green suit, and the helmet lay on the table beside him. He smiled with his mouth, but there was no warmth in his eyes.

"On your own, Ondray?"

"I wanted to talk to you face to face. No third parties to confuse the issue."

"Not even your wife?"

He refused to acknowledge that Hoopa's jealousy could really be responsible for any of this. The man was just having a dig at the most famous terrie-loonie liaison on Mars.

"Someone has to keep things ticking over at New Tycho."

"So what do you want to discuss?"

"Tolly, you're not stupid. You *know* we can't recall the Ship. Tell the people here you made a mistake. Encourage them to put down roots on Mars. A lot of them look up to you—"it was an unfortunate choice of phrase, with Hoopa still smiling down at him from his loonie height "—for some reason. I'm going to need someone to run things here. Why not you?"

"They just want to go home, Ondray. Nobody explained how hard it would be here. How long it would take. Nobody listens to them any more. At least, nobody does anything. Mandelbrot listens, but that's all."

"Forget Mandelbrot. I'll listen, and I'll take any action within reason to make people happy. But recalling the Ship isn't just unreasonable, it's impossible."

"So you keep telling us. And now you've come to take me back to New Tycho with you, so that I can be persuaded to see reason. Then, no doubt, you'll bring me back here to explain your point of view to my people."

It was so close to Ondray's original plan that he felt uncomfortable. But now he had something else—an ace in the hole.

"Not quite, Tolly. I've got something to show you. A surprise. If it doesn't make you think again, nothing will. But whether you think again or not, I *can't* recall the Ship. You know that."

Hoopa picked up his helmet.

"Well, what are we waiting for? I've no objection to visiting New Tycho. Perhaps I might even be allowed to meet your wife. I'm sure she can be much more persuasive than you are. And you and I can talk just as well in the rover as we can here."

Thirteen

THE YELLOW COVERALL FELT SCRATCHY ON HIS SKIN, AND even the soft slippers seemed to be rubbing his heels as he walked. But Ondray supposed that was the price you had to pay for a brand new body, not yet hardened and calloused by the rough and tumble of everyday life. At least he was no longer thirsty, and the pleasure of eating the simple meal that the Ship had prepared for him had been the first thing that had suggested to him there were advantages in being human again.

But the taste of the food wasn't enough to make him want to extend his stay here. He had two tasks. First, to check that the body really was working properly, then to make sure that the Protector fully accepted him as a competent human being. If necessary, he'd take that ridiculous Test again—the Test he had taken, in his original body, when he and Tugela had broken into the Ship, all those years ago, and re-established human control over the Protector after millennia of separation. But he didn't really expect it to be necessary.

He had walked the short distance from the new hibernation unit along the gently curving corridor, ending in a seemingly blank wall. Time to check that the interface was still working.

Open up, Link.

A crack appeared in the wall, and the door slid sideways. He stepped out into the inner world of the Ship.

In front of him, a seemingly immense space stretched away into the distance, starkly contrasting with the claustrophobic confines of the narrow corridor. To either side, the floor curved away, rising until the two sides met in arch overhead.

It was all, like the artefacts that covered the floor, familiar and comforting. He smiled, as he remembered the first time that he had stood at a doorway like this, with Tugela, terrified at the strangeness of the surroundings, trying desperately not to show his fear. He took a deep breath, savouring the oxygen rich air—air boosted from the old Lunar normal to a much richer, thicker mix (though still some way short of Earth normal) solely for his benefit. A far cry, indeed, from his first visit.

He looked to his right, up the curving floor/wall. Somewhere up there, about 30 degrees round, was the old hibernation unit where fifteen pods, seven of them occupied, and a network of computer systems housed the entity that had been, and in a sense was still, the Protector. An intelligence created out of the merging of the original Protector's mind with those of the semi-autonomous hibernation systems and six loonie refugees, plus what was left of the Planner himself, the person who had designed this Ship.

When he was part of the Link, the Protector seemed to Ondray like a red-orange ball, somewhere at the base of his spine. It had once been a counterpart to the Link itself; now, the two intelligences tolerated each other in the Ship's systems. Link had the upper hand; there was no prospect of a disagreement that would threaten the running of the Ship's systems.

But that upper hand depended, to an extent that neither Link nor Ondray could be sure, on the Protector's inbuilt imperative to live up to its name—to protect human beings. It was the presence of Ondray that had tipped the balance and enabled Link to gain control of the Ship; and the continued presence of Ondray, even a copy of Ondray, was their insurance that the status quo would be maintained.

He looked back out, beyond the clutter of artefacts, to the glinting band of water, the cylindrical lake that circled the Ship and provided reaction mass for the auxiliary drive. Overhead, the "sky" was striped with bands of dark blue, with the stripes in between producing a diffuse yellowish light. And exactly halfway between the "sky" and the "ground" there was a long, thin streak, the central pipe that carried essential service ducts from one end of the Ship to the other, running off into the distance. It was held in place by three spokes, even thinner than the pipe, radiating out to meet the wall of the habitat.

The whole cylinder, Ondray knew, was rotating, so that everything on the inner surface was pressed outwards with the equivalent of lunar normal gravity. Climb up one of those spokes, as he once had, and "gravity" would seem to decrease steadily, fading away to nothing at all at the central axis of the cylinder. But he had no intention of ever doing *that* climb again.

This was far enough. The body worked; the interface worked. Just a couple of checks with the Protector, and he could get out of these itchy clothes, out of his achy body, and return to the cozy familiarity of the Link. He knew that Link was in the circuit, so there seemed little doubt that the Protector would be eavesdropping, even though he never initiated a discussion.

Protector, I am testing this circuit. Do you read me?
YES.

63

Ever since the reunion, the modified Protector had only responded to direct questions or commands.

Who am I?

YOU ARE ONDRAY.

Where am I?

YOU ARE STANDING OUTSIDE THE ENTRANCE TO CORRIDOR SEVEN, ON LEVEL ONE.

Please confirm my status. It did no harm to be polite, even if the machine had no feelings. And this, after all, was the big one.

YOU ARE A COMPETENT HUMAN BEING.

A wave of relief swept through Ondray. That was it. A competent human being was one that had passed the Protector's—originally the Planner's—Test, designed to stop children and incompetents from issuing orders that machine intelligences would obey unhesitatingly, even if they were damaging to the habitat. The Protector had to *protect* all human life (although it had proved capable of some fancy interpretation of what that imperative meant), but it only had to *obey* competent human beings. It had accepted that this combination of Ondray's persona and the clone body was indeed a competent human being.

Now he could dump the clone body back in the hibernation unit, and hope that he never needed to use it again. Link must have guessed what was in his mind, although he'd been careful not to express the thought directly.

I'd like you to run a few more tests, Ondray, if you don't mind.

What kind of tests?

Perhaps you could ride up to the Command Centre, check that the emergency systems are responding satisfactorily.

He sighed. What Link meant, of course, was that they ought to check that the systems really did respond to Ondray's voice, in the new body, as well as to the interface.

He couldn't imagine an emergency that would leave those old systems, the last of the many backups, still functioning, and the Protector still able to respond to them, even though the interface and, by implication, Link himself, had gone from the system.

But then, who could have imagined the importance of those old voice operated systems in his first blundering attempts to gain control over the Protector, on their first encounter? He supposed it was his duty. And Ondray had always been good about doing his duty.

At least, this time he wouldn't have to make the journey the hard way.

Protector: Fetch me the carrier.

While he was waiting, he looked out again to the far end of the cylinder, at the big central dome, surrounded by structures large enough to be seen even at this distance. The Command Centre, repaired after his original violent entry through the roof of the dome. The original nerve centre of the Ship, back when it had been built as a habitat in Earth orbit.

Why on Earth, he wondered incongruously, *couldn't they have built it next to the hibernation units?*

He must have allowed the thought to be expressed too clearly in his conscious mind. Link picked it up, and responded.

Safety, Ondray. Separate vital systems as much as possible. But don't worry. It won't take more than a few hours. And we've plenty of time before we reach the comet belt.

Fourteen

DURING THE EARLY PART OF THE TRIP BACK TO NEW TYCHO, Ondray almost began to wonder whether he had read Tolly correctly. The loonie seemed completely unconcerned by his virtual arrest, and although uncommunicative seemed happy to help out with the routine, preparing a simple meal which they shared while the rover rolled along on autopilot. He almost seemed happy to be being taken away from Terranova.

Ondray continued to worry over the point when they stopped and prepared to bed down for their brief overnight halt. He lay down in his bunk determined to worry his way through the growing sense of unease to find out what it was that his subconscious was trying to tell him. But he must have been more exhausted by the events of the day than he realised. The next thing he knew, he was being roused from sleep, struggling dozily towards consciousness, by a soft drumming noise.

A malfunction? Something wrong with the air supply? He was wide awake, reaching for his suit, when he realised. The sound was coming from outside, muffled by the double hull. Something was tapping against the outer surface of the vehicle.

It couldn't be a comet; there was nothing due for months. Debris from a volcanic eruption?

"Tolly! Get out of there! Move! Suit up!"

While he roused the still sleepy loonie from his bunk, he was stepping into his own suit. How could there have been an eruption? Mars was geologically dead. And if there had been an eruption, surely ground tremors would have woken them before the fallout started pattering on the hull of the rover?

Still tugging at the fastenings of the suit, he leaned forward over the seat in the bubble at the front of the vehicle, and hit the control for the main lights.

He froze, stunned. Large raindrops were falling lazily through the beam of the lights in the low gravity, sending up spurts of dust as they splashed onto the surface outside. *It was raining*. Not a lot; not teeming torrents of water falling from the sky. But real rain, on Mars. *He had been woken by the sound of rain on the roof.*

Ondray found his voice. "Look at this, Tolly. Here's something to make your farmers think again."

The loonie, fully suited, helmet in his hand, pressed forward alongside him, gazing out through the bubble. For the first time, his air of smug self-assurance seemed to waver.

"I never expected . . ."

Then he seemed to deliberately take a grip on his emotions.

"It's too late. This changes nothing, Ondray. How many more years before there are *reliable* rains? Before rivers flow?" He paused. "There is one thing it changes."

Ondray turned his head to look at Tolly. "Yes?"

Tolly nodded towards the brightly lit scene outside. "Much more of that, and the track will wash away. Hadn't we better get this thing moving?"

Disappointed at Tolly's reaction, but still excited at the rainfall, Ondray had to agree. Even though the shower was already showing signs of stopping, there was no telling how badly affected the surface was. It was only a couple of hours until dawn, anyway; with two of them, it would be safe to press on, slowly, as far as possible before the Sun rose, saving as much daylight as possible to help them negotiate any changes that had occurred in the terrain, changes which would not, of course, be known to the autopilot.

He called New Tycho, let them know his plans. There had been no rain there. It must have been an isolated shower. But there had been lightning to the southwest of the city. *If there's one shower*, Ondray told himself, *there must be more.*

Aloud, he simply said "we're on our way, Tolly. And I've still got something even better to show you, just down the road." There was no response, but his companion slid into the right hand seat, watchful, alert to any dangers on the road ahead.

Progress was slow. Several times, they had to make minor diversions. But as the Sun came up their pace increased. Allowing for the fact that they had started so early, they were ahead of Ondray's original schedule; there would be plenty of time for a demonstration of the tenacity of life on Mars, and they'd still get back to New Tycho around dusk.

Ondray recognised some of the scenery, and the autopilot had every bizarrely shaped outcrop of rock along the route locked in its memory. They were just a few minutes away from the spot where he had seen the plant when they rounded a bend, weaving between two pillars of rock that towered over the rover, and saw the destruction ahead. He reached for the controls, but the safeties had already cut in, stopping the vehicle a good ten meters short of the fall. One of the towering spires had fallen, completely blocking the road. Beyond, the cliff to the left of the road had slumped, sending a wave of mud across their path. To the right, a forest of rocky spires still stood, like the pillars of some ancient, roofless building. It would be possible, carefully, to pick a way through the spires, round the obstructions and back on to the road to New Tycho. But Ondray was sure that this was where he had stopped on the outward journey. The mound he had climbed was part of that mud slide ahead; the crack in the rock, the frost hollow where he had seen the plant, was—he couldn't quite be sure—it was either buried in the mud or under the rocks of that fallen spire.

"What happened? I thought we were clear of the shower region?"

"If there's one shower, Tolly, there's bound to be more. I told you. The climate's changing. Just our bad luck that there's been some heavy rain here, right where we want to go."

"That rock fall doesn't look like the work of rain."

"How the hell do I know?" Ondray's anger exploded. "Maybe it was struck by lightning. Maybe it's been balancing there for aeons, ready to fall, and the rain was the last straw. This planet's *changing*, Tolly. Don't you understand? Don't you want to be part of it?"

"I want to go home, Ondray. That's what I understand. That's what the people want."

Ondray slid out of the seat, tugged Tolly by the shoulder. "Get out of there. Get your helmet on. I want to show you something." Tolly shrugged, visible even through his suit, and rose out of his seat. He seemed amused. *I'll make him laugh on the other side of his face*, Ondray thought, wrenching his own helmet into position, heading for the airlock.

It was a useless gesture, but the physical exercise helped him to calm down. They scrambled over the smaller pieces of rock, Tolly following obediently but offering no comment;

but he could see nothing resembling the kloof where he had found the frost hollow. At the edge of the mud slide, he went as far as sticking one booted foot forward into the sticky mess, then reason returned.

He stopped, pulled the foot back and stood, panting, gazing out at the new landscape. His brain started working normally again.

This stuff's barely above freezing, even now; it'll be solid, tonight. It was, obviously, only thanks to the latent heat released on condensing out, or freezing, in the clouds that had made the showers fall as rain rather than snow. It would, indeed, be a long time yet before the farmers saw rivers flowing across this still barren land. He kicked at the setting mud wall.

"What do you want to show me, Ondray?" Tolly seemed amused.

"It doesn't matter."

He turned, stumped back towards the rover. Nothing mattered. Except, somehow, to make the farmers see reason.

Automatically, he went through the cleanup routine in the airlock, and opened the inner door. A red light was flashing, persistently, on the control panel. In his haste to get Tolly out of the vehicle, he had neglected to patch the comlink through to their suits.

Dropping his helmet on the bunk, he stumbled forward, almost tripping over his own feet, still encased in their thermal outdoor boots. Once again, he leaned over the seat, stabbed at the panel.

The screen lit to show Tugela's worried face, turned to one side, checking something out of camera range. As her panel indicated that he was answering her call, she turned, still sober faced, to look straight out as him. There was no friendly greeting. She simply said, "Ondray. We have a problem."

Fifteen

IT WAS COMETS THAT HAD BROUGHT LIFE TO THE PLANET in the first place, more than four billion years ago. Comets depositing their burden of ice to make the waters that covered the Earth, and depositing with the ice organic material, complex molecules that had formed over long aeons of time in interstellar clouds, and which became even more complex in the environment of the warm little ponds that formed from the water brought to Earth by the comets.

From time to time comets had also brought death to the planet, most notably some 65 million years ago, when many species of life on Earth had been wiped out in the aftermath of a series of major cometary impacts, impacts that had thrown debris into the air, darkening the skies and bringing the long winter.

But life was resilient. It always recovered from these setbacks. Indeed, the notable thing about the impacts at 65 Myr wasn't their size—there had been even bigger disasters in the past—but the way in which life recovered. Recovered, and, eventually, learned to use comets to its own advantage, taking life, as a result, out from the Earth, first to its nearest neighbour, the Moon, and then on to Mars.

It was unfortunate that something had disturbed the belt of debris, out beyond Neptune, where the comets came from. Unfortunate that there were now too many comets coming in to the inner Solar System for the *Perseus* probes to control. It was inevitable that some of these comets should strike the Earth itself. But the planet was large, and the Islands to which civilization was now confined were small. Several small comets had already impacted in different parts of the world, bringing local destruction, and causing some climatic problems, but nothing to worry the Islands in the short term. All would be well, as long as the Sun itself soon returned to normal, and the Ship solved the long term problem of the disturbance in the comet belt.

At least the people of the Islands had good information about the kind of debris falling in to their part of the Solar System. Most of the incoming cometary nuclei were small—far smaller than the chunks of interplanetary debris that had finished off the dinosaurs. And most of them were not even on intersecting orbits with the Earth. It would be extremely bad luck if anything untoward were to happen to the Islands themselves. But bad luck, as the dinosaurs had discovered, did happen, from time to time.

Sixteen

"WHAT KIND OF A PROBLEM?"

"Terranova. And here. Some of the farmers have taken the two shuttles. They're in orbit, at the satellite. They've cut the comlink with Earth."

Both shuttles? With hindsight, he could understand Tolly's complacent acceptance of his captive status. Obviously, this had been planned. He had enough followers at Terranova for some ridiculous act of defiance like this. There had been no guards on the spacecraft, after all. Why should there have been? But *both* shuttles?

He swung sideways. "What's going on, Tolly?"

"Surprised, Ondray? Surprised that I have just a few followers even in New Tycho? Perhaps there are more people eager to go home than you realise."

He swung back to the screen.

"What about the orbiting shuttle? Have you called it down?"

"No response. They got to it before anyone knew what was going on."

"That's ridiculous. Someone *must* have noticed. Were you all asleep?"

She shook her head. She looked close to tears.

"Not asleep, Ondray. Distracted. That isn't the worst of it."

Not the worst? Cut off from communication with Earth—and, he realised belatedly, cut off from communication *through* Earth to the Ship—without any access to the remaining shuttles, and she said that wasn't the worst?

He saw Tolly out of the corner of his eye, now in the seat alongside him again, smiling broadly. Tugela was still speaking.

"Mandelbrot got wind of what was going on. He tried to stop them. There's been fighting at Terranova. And sabotage. Mandelbrot got things under control, but the rebels blew up the air compressors. *Both* air compressors."

Tolly's smile vanished. "That's wrong. Impossible. It was just a bluff . . . I *told* Rikkard. Just a bluff . . ."

"What the comet is going on, Tolly? It doesn't sound like any kind of a bluff to me. You're behind this; what's it all for?"

Some of the loonie's bluster returned. "It's simple, Ondray. We decided to take a leaf out of the Protector's book. Remember how he cut off communications with the Moon, forced us to re-establish contact with Earth ourselves?"

That wasn't quite the way Ondray remembered it, but never mind. He nodded.

"We've done the same thing. Cut off communications. Earth will report the problem to the Ship. The Ship will have no choice but to come back and find out what's gone wrong. The Prime Directive. And once it's here, it might as well ferry us back to the Moon before it heads off into deep space again. *If* it heads off into deep space again." The hint of returning bluster faded. "Only . . ." "Only what, Tolly?" Damn it, it might just work. The Prime Directive was a strong influence on the Link, as well as on the Protector.

76

The best hope was that his twin self would somehow be able to override the directive.

"Only there wasn't supposed to be any bloodshed. There are enough people who want to go home to overwhelm any organised opposition at Terranova peacefully. They were just supposed to take the shuttles and cut the comlink. Three people in each shuttle; I told them to stay in orbit until the Ship returns, not to listen to any messages from down here."

"And on the ground?"

"Rikkard was supposed to *threaten* to blow the compressors, if anyone got rough. Only *threaten*, you understand? A bluff."

Tugela intervened. "Mandelbrot called that bluff, Tolly."

"Then Mandelbrot's a fool."

"*Was* a fool. He died in the blast. So did Rikkard. So did thirty-one other people."

Ondray remembered his last view of Mandelbrot, shoulders slumped, walking away down the corridor. The message must have got through, all right. The old hero had remembered his duty, after all. But too late.

"Who's in charge there now?"

"Hoffa."

"How long have they got?"

She shrugged. "Hard to say. They lost a lot of air from Dome Two before the damage was repaired. All the rovers are out of action; sabotaged, I think. It's all still a bit confused. But there's emergency oxygen in their rovers and suit tanks, at least enough to help the injured."

"Injured?"

"What do you expect, Ondray? There was a bloody explosion out there."

While he'd been prancing about outside, looking for flowers, having forgotten to switch the circuit over.

"Sorry. How long?"

"Maybe forty-eight hours, before the weakest start to suffer."

"OK. Wait." He turned to Tolly again. There was no trace of a smirk on the loonie's lips now; indeed, he looked pale, worried. "Do you want those farmers to die, Tolly?"

He shook his head.

"Then call those shuttles down. Order them to pick up a compressor from New Tycho, and ferry it to Terranova. I'll even let them go back up to orbit afterwards, if that's what it takes to make you see sense."

He shook his head again.

"They won't do it. They won't even be listening. I told them to leave the ground-to-ground link functioning, so that you could talk to Terranova, know that what I told you was the truth. But I also told them to shut down their receivers. I didn't want any chance of you bluffing them back down here."

It was, Ondray realised, a backhanded kind of compliment to his own known negotiating skills. But that was no comfort. "Try, dammit."

"Oh, I'll try. But it won't do any good. We're on our own, now. At least, until the Ship returns."

And that could be a very long wait. On their own. The irony struck Ondray with full force. He'd got what he wanted—but not the way he'd wanted.

There was only one chance.

"OK, Tugela. Get a spare compressor loaded on to a trailer and head on out to meet us."

She smiled, weakly. "It's almost ready, Ondray. There's just about enough time."

He nodded. Of course she had started the ball rolling, even while doubtless worried sick at his failure to respond to her calls. "We'll be a little slow—the terrain has changed a lot round here, and we'll be on manual for quite a while yet. But we'll meet you as close as we can to halfway between here and New Tycho. At least then this vehicle will have an up to date memory of the route; we can swap the trailer over and head back at full speed on auto—through the night, if necessary. And while we're on our way, you can beam Tolly up to the comsat. Maybe somebody up there will decide not to follow orders."

Tolly shook his head, but said nothing. *Yeah*, Ondray thought. *We're dealing with fanatics, here. If anyone up there is disobeying orders, then judging by what's happened at Terranova it'll be in the opposite direction. They won't be keeping the channels open, but smashing the communications gear into tiny pieces.*

Seventeen

"ONDRAY, WE HAVE A PROBLEM."

The words came over the speakers in the old Command Centre, not over the interface. He looked up from the control panel, muscles tensing, hair rising at the back of his neck. This organic body was so bloody vulnerable. He wondered how long it would take him to get back to the hibernation unit, and get his mind back into the safety of the Link systems. But everything *looked* normal.

"What kind of a problem, Link?"

"Nothing to do with the Ship." He relaxed. "It's a communications difficulty. R'apehu has just informed us that they have lost contact with Mars."

Lost contact with Mars? It was impossible.

"What do they mean?"

"Just what they say. The link went down. Cut dead, with no warning. No emergency messages before, and nothing at all since."

"So what do we do?" His mind was racing through the possibilities. A comet strike, wiping out both colonies at once? Surely impossible—and any incoming comets would have been noticed weeks in advance. A problem with the comsat? Possible, but unlikely. He gave up, listened to Link's reply.

"Nothing, at present. R'apehu is trying to re-establish contact. It may be only a minor problem. But if it persists, we may have to make a decision."

"Decision? What decision?"

"Human lives may be in danger, Ondray." Oh no. Not *that* again. He let go of the hand grips, floating away from the control panel. Here, on the axis of the Ship, there was no centrifugal force to create the illusion of gravity, and he'd been happy to leave the local artificial gravity turned off, resting the tired muscles of his new body.

"Link, the whole purpose of this mission is to reduce the danger to human lives." He knew he was speaking for the benefit of the Protector, who must be aware of the conversation, and the events leading up to it.

"Yes. But there will be no point in solving the comet problem if there is nobody left alive on Mars to benefit."

"There are many more people on Earth who need our help in solving the comet problem."

"Yes. As I said, there is no need for any action yet. On balance, it is clear that we must proceed with the mission. But I need to ask you a favour."

"Go ahead." He could guess what was coming.

"Perhaps you wouldn't mind staying in your present body until the situation is resolved."

"Yeah." Since, if it came right down to the wire, they could still rely on the Protector obeying the direct orders of a competent human being.

"Just one request in return, Link."

"Anything in my power, Ondray."

"Get me a full suit, with air tanks, and a helmet. I'll stay up here for a while, but if there are any more surprises, I want to be able to get back to the hibernation unit under my own power, under any circumstances."

"I understand. You won't need it, I'm sure. But I'll get it for you anyway. At once."

He hoped he wouldn't need it, either. But if the debate between Link and the Protector got too fierce, and between them they managed to neglect the life support systems while they slugged it out inside the Ship's systems, he wanted to be able to look after himself.

"And another thing, Link." He half smiled at an old memory. "Get me some more food, and water. If I'm stuck in this body for a while, I'd better look after it."

Eighteen

"I THINK WE'RE COMING OUT OF IT."

Ondray, his gaze fixed on the next obstacle to be negotiated, hadn't noticed any change in the longer perspective; but Tolly, coming back from preparing some food in one of the breaks from his almost incessant calling of the satellite, could look further ahead, to more open territory.

"Good." Ondray didn't take his eyes off the path he was negotiating between two rocky outcrops, but as he rounded the rock pillar on his left and saw a short stretch of clear terrain ahead he reached with one hand for the ration bar and munched it, tasting nothing, while he steered one-handed for a while.

Ten hours, he thought. *Ten bloody hours. It's about time we were coming out of it.*

The hours spent grinding slowly through the "petrified forest" of rock pillars had passed painfully slowly, in spite of the intense concentration required to pick out the safe route. Ondray kept reminding himself that it didn't really matter how long they took, that the rover from New Tycho towing a trailer with the relief equipment was heading towards them as fast as it could anyway, that all he and Tolly had to do was get clear of the messy terrain and back on to their proper route in time to link up with the party from New Tycho. Swap the trailer over, and then they could sleep all the way back to Terranova, if they wanted to, with the new route safely programmed into what passed for their rover's brain. While Ondray drove, Tolly was at the com link, trying to get through to the rebels up at the satellite. It was, as he had predicted, to no avail. Either they had disabled the receiving equipment, or, thanks to Tolly's careful coaching in the whiles of Ondray, they believed his messages to be some sort of a trick. Either way, there was no acknowledgement. Clearly, nothing short of the return of the Ship to Mars orbit would persuade them to return to the surface of the planet But Tolly seemed sincerely concerned, and they kept the link to the satellite open, just in case. The duty engineer in the comcentre at New Tycho stayed in the circuit, keeping them informed, from time to time, of the progress of the relief rover.

But still, ten hours and they hadn't yet cleared the pillared terrain. Another couple of hours before they could make the swap; then, with a trailer in tow, even with a route known to the rover it was going to be nearly as long getting back through the pillars to the mud slide. And all the while, people could be dying out at Terranova.

He rubbed the back of his hand, still holding a half-eaten food bar, across his tired eyes. Tolly was right; it *was* getting clearer. Clear enough, in fact, for him to take both hands off the controls and stretch his aching back.

"Take over, Tolly." Somehow, he could no longer regard his companion as in any sense a prisoner. They were in this together now, with a common interest in helping the stricken Terranova colony. "It's no use calling the satellite again. I'm going to rest for an hour; there'll be plenty to do when we meet up with the others."

The hour had stretched to nearly 150 minutes when Ondray was woken from deep sleep by Tolly shaking his shoulder.

"I can see their lights, Ondray. We've made the linkup."

Lights? Of course; it was fully dark by now. Ondray's brain cleared as he swung his feet off the bunk and on to the floor of the rover.

"Any news?"

"None from the satellite." Tolly knew where Ondray's priorities now lay. "Much the same at Terranova."

Much the same. Probably meaning another couple of people had died, but nobody wanted to burden Ondray with the details. They meant well enough, though. Not worth worrying him when he could do no more than he was already doing to help.

He stood up, moved back into the left hand seat in the front bubble. They were on the main track, moving at a good pace; and there were indeed lights, lights that could only be those of the relief rover, approaching, fast.

The com link, showing a blank screen, was still hooked through New Tycho to the satellite; the engineer would be listening in. He touched a control under the screen.

"Patch me through to the other rover."

The screen flickered and cleared.

Tugela! Looking tired, worried, but beautiful. For a moment, he thought the engineer had misunderstood, and had put him through to the administration unit in New Tycho, then, as she smiled in recognition, he saw the familiar background of a rover interior behind her.

The idiot. Even while he thought it, he felt more relaxed than he had done since news of the rebellion first reached him. *She ought to be tucked up in bed.* But he smiled in return, delighted at the prospect of seeing her, not just on screen but in the flesh, in a few more minutes.

"Surprised, Ondray?"

"There was no need, Tugela. Anybody could have brought the trailer out."

"Would you rather I'd stayed behind?"

It scarcely took a moment's thought. If he *had* thought about it, he would have *ordered* her to stay behind. She'd be more use than Tarragon if another emergency blew up. Of course, she'd known that—which was why no hint that she was on board the other rover had reached him. Tugela always had been good at getting her own way. She *ought* to have stayed behind, sure. But he'd much *rather* she was here, with him, now.

He shook his head, still smiling broadly.

"I'd rather have you here. But there's work to do; can't stay long."

Her smile faded. "I know. But I had to see you, Ondray. Talk to you before you turn back." Talk to you *personally*, was what she clearly meant, not over a com link with anyone on Mars listening in. He felt the same. "See you outside then. In ten minutes?"

She looked at something on her control panel, out of range of the view on his screen.

"Seven, at the rate you're going now. OK?"

"OK. I'll suit up."

He cut the connection, and turned to Tolly.

There was no smile on the face of his companion.

"You really care for her, don't you, Ondray?"

He shrugged, feeling the smile fade, but still feeling ridiculously lighthearted in spite of his fatigue.

"Of course."

"And she does for you."

There was a silence.

"Maybe I've been wrong about more than one thing. You'd better suit up. I'll handle things in here." And with that his attention was back on the controls, getting ready to bring the rover to a halt on a broad patch of level ground that was clearly visible in their lights.

Ondray stood, moved towards the rear of the vehicle. His mind was whirling. So Tolly *had* resented his marriage to Tugela; and yet, he now seemed to be saying he regretted his jealousy. Was this whole business, including the rebellion, tangled up in some imagined personal rivalry with Ondray?

He opened his mouth to speak, then closed it, shaking his head gently. Better to say nothing, now. Perhaps not ever. Suit up, and get on with the job of rebuilding the colony—*together*. Aware of his adrenaline-fuelled surge of alertness, eager to get out of the rover and meet up with Tugela, Ondray took several deep breaths, and forced himself to suit up carefully, checking everything, and double-checking. No point in getting out there 40 seconds quicker but with the suit not properly sealed. Especially at this time of night.

The rover stopped, then shunted back and forth a little, so that he had to fling out one hand for support against the wall. Then it was stopped properly, and he was dressed in the yellow suit, helmet on, cycling through the airlock.

As he stepped out, he saw in the lights the other rover, already parked, with two figures, one in red and the other in a blue suit, working at the trailer connection. And he saw a familiar tall figure in a green suit, halfway towards him from the other vehicle.

At last, caution went out of the window. He broke into the loping run that gave the best speed under Martian gravity. Her voice, relayed through the com link in the rover, reached him as he ran.

"What took you so long?"

"Ran into some bad weather. How about you?"

But now they were together, and there was no need for talk. She held out both her hands, and he clung on to them, gripping tightly, as he came to a halt. He couldn't see much of her face, with the light reflecting off her helmet, and they were holding hands through two layers of pressure suit. But still, it beat the com link. And still, there was work to do.

Over the open communications channel, he heard one of Tugela's crew—it sounded like Kavaney—talking to Tolly.

"Can you confirm the status of your vehicle?"

"We've got air for more than 40 hours; should be ample. It can't possibly take more than 30 to get back to Terranova."

"Fuel?"

"No problem. Looks as if it was topped up at Terranova during Ondray's visit."

"OK."

"How long before we can turn around?"

The answer came from another male voice, one he didn't recognise, presumably the other one of the two figures working on the trailer connection.

"We're just about clear here. I'll move our rover out of the way, then you can back up and latch on. Ten minutes?"

Ten minutes! And then separation for another couple of days.

Tugela had let go of his left hand, and was tugging him with the other, towards the now-unhitched rover.

"Come on. They know what they are doing."

The figure in the red suit was entering the rover, outer airlock door closing behind him; the one in blue stood by the trailer. He raised an arm in greeting as they reached the back of the vehicle. Ondray barely had time to acknowledge the gesture, then the outer airlock door was opening again and Tugela was pulling him up inside, hitting the control to close the outer door as soon as they were across the threshold.

Somebody hasn't been following regulations, thought Ondray. There clearly hadn't been time for the red-suited figure to clean the dust off before going on into the interior of the vehicle. But if it gave him a minute or two in private with Tugela, he wasn't going to complain.

She was removing her helmet, gesturing to him to do the same. He did so, as the vehicle lurched forward, moving out of the way so that Tolly could hitch the other rover to the trailer.

Now, he could see her face. She looked more beautiful than ever, eyes bright, panting slightly from her exertions. She slid to the floor, sitting cross legged, patting the space beside her. Automatically, he followed suit; they always sat, if possible, when they were together; it helped to cancel out the height difference.

She leaned forward and kissed him, gently.

"Don't look so puzzled, love. We aren't kidnapping you. I just wanted to talk, in private." No com link; no chance of anyone eavesdropping, by accident or design.

"But even if we can't kidnap you, I wanted to ask if you really have to go back to Terranova. I've got Kavaney and Pylar with me; both good drivers. Let them take the equipment on."

He shook his head.

"I have to go. With Tolly. It's the only way to sort this mess out. I think he's seen reason, and they'll listen to him. But I have to be there to make sure. And I have to be there anyway, where the problems are. Nobody's going to think much of me if I lock myself away in New Tycho at the first sign of trouble. I *have* to go. Is that why you wanted a private talk? Did you think you could persuade me otherwise?"

She looked down.

"No. I had to ask. For myself. Everybody knows you run towards problems, not away from them. I was just being selfish. I knew what you would say. I know you're right. But I had to ask."

He reached for her hand, and leaned forward. They kissed again, as she put her arm around him.

"A good excuse for a private meeting, though," he murmured.

"I've got a better excuse than that, love." He knew she was smiling, even though he couldn't see her face. But that was all she said. His head, nestled beneath hers, moved with the soft rise and fall of her chest; he could hear the steady beat of her heart. Time seemed to stand still. Surely, the ten minutes must be up by now? Equally surely, though, none of the others would enter this airlock until he opened the door. But, just for that reason, he had to resist the temptation to stay a minute longer than necessary. If rank had its privileges, it also had its duties.

Reluctantly, he pulled away from her a little, looked into her eyes.

"I have to go."

He kissed her again, lightly. No point in rousing passions that could not be fulfilled for another three days.

"Don't you want my news, then?" She was playing games with him, laughing inwardly at some secret. He almost began to be annoyed. She shouldn't really have come out here, distracting him from the work in hand. The story would be all over the colony, doubtless highly embroidered, by the time he got back.

She must have sensed his irritation. The smile on her lips faded, though her eyes still seemed to shine. She lifted a finger to his lips.

"No, Ondray; it really is important. I wanted you to know at once, but I don't want the whole of Mars to know yet." She paused. "I'm pregnant."

He sat, astonished, for a full five seconds. Then he leaned forward, wrapping both his arms around her slim body, trying to think of the right words. The terranovans would just have to wait another minute or so for their relief.

Nineteen

THE *PERSEUS* CRAFT HAD DONE THEIR WORK WELL, WITHIN the limitations imposed by their manouvering systems and the laws of physics. Most of the cometary debris shaken loose from the trans-Neptunian belt could be ignored; it would make for a spectacular display in the skies of the inner planets, but posed no direct threat. A couple of the comets could, even now, be directed towards Mars, to give a boost to the terraforming efforts there, without distracting from what was now the probes' key priority. But their over-riding imperative was now to minimise the risk to Earth.

Three cometary nuclei on trajectories that threatened to intersect with the Earth-Moon system had already been deflected. It was just unfortunate that the fourth had broken apart under the strain, while the *Perseus* craft were pushing it on to a safer path. There were simply too many fragments remaining to do much with, in the time available; and if the *Perseus* probes had stayed with the fragmenting comet to take care of every last chunk of ice, they would have fallen too far in towards the Sun to be able to get back to their proper orbits in time to deal with the next interloper.

The largest fragments, at least, were safely dealt with. All that was left was the cosmic equivalent of buckshot, a few chunks of ice each comparable in size to a large mountain on Earth, spreading gently apart as they moved on slightly different trajectories, but falling more or less together towards the double planet. Such a chunk of ice, entering the Earth's atmosphere at high speed, would heat up and explode in the air before it could reach the ground. It would make no crater, although it might, at worst, produce a blast sufficient to knock over the trees in a forest, or destroy buildings, over an area tens of kilometers across. It would be very unfortunate if any city were directly underneath such a blast; but there were very few cities on Earth, any more, and the chance was remote.

Long before the cometary debris reached the Earth, it had grown a huge tail as material boiled off from the icy fragments in the heat of the Sun. Even in daytime, the comet showed in the sky, like a pale Moon; at night, the streamers of material pointing away from the Sun stretched halfway across the sky. Stars, faintly visible through the cometary tail, showed to anyone who cared to look, just how insubstantial the tail was, and how little of the original ice had evaporated from the chunks forming the loose nucleus.

But the people of the Islands were unworried. The closer the cloud of cosmic buckshot got, the more accurate, and the more reassuring, the projections of its trajectory became. The ice mountains would scatter themselves uncomfortably close to the Islands, but definitely to the north, over the open ocean.

Just one stray fragment from the swarm, one mountain of ice, came in on a trajectory almost over the northernmost tip of the Islands. After all, one fragment in the cloud, by definition, had to be the southernmost. All of the people on the northern island had retreated southward, as a matter of course, and taken shelter, just in case. So when the explosion occurred, equivalent to the blast of a moderate sized nuclear bomb, but without the accompanying radiation, no human lives were lost.

Of course, there was damage. Even with the partial shelter provided by the mountains, many farms were destroyed, and there was severe destruction in three small northern towns. The full brunt of the blast, though, was felt on the mountain top at R'apehu. The old observatory was completely destroyed.

It would be several months before the finger of laser light would stab out from the mountain top once again, conveying its messages to be relayed around the Solar System. But, naturally, rebuilding the human habitations had to take priority. There was nothing anyone on Earth could do for the Martians, even if they were in contact; and, besides, all the evidence suggested that the Martians themselves had deliberately broken contact, well before the comet fragment had wreaked its destruction.

As for the Ship—well, that was a long shot anyway, and well out of terrestrial control. They would either succeed, or fail, regardless of events at home.

Earth first was the guiding principle when the reconstruction work began. They had, after all, seemingly weathered the cosmic storm; maybe the cometary threat was diminishing of its own accord. The Martian colony had been a drain on scarce resources, resources that would have been invaluable in the present reconstruction. No, the com link could wait. Earth came first.

Twenty

ONDRAY'S BREATHING WAS LOUD IN HIS EARS AS HE MOVED cautiously, hand over hand, along the line of evenly spaced rungs. Under gravity, or if the Ship was accelerating, it would be a ladder. But the drive had been turned off for his excursion outside, and would stay off until he returned to the interior of the vessel. Even the spin had been stopped, so that there was no risk of him being flung away into space. Weightless, he drifted along the ladder at a steady speed, padding gently at the rungs with alternate hands—a left, and a right, and a left, and . . .

The rhythm was hypnotic, and he made himself stop and wait for a moment, taking stock of his surroundings. Behind him, the long snake of a safety line stretched back to the airlock. Above—the Ship was so big that this close, even in weightless conditions it was easy to convince his mind that "down" was towards the hull—the stars shone diamond bright, unflickering against the black backdrop.

Only another 20 meters or so away, along the ladder, was the cluster of antennas representing the business end of the main com link.

He shouldn't really be out here, as the Protector had repeatedly reminded him. The robots might not be very bright, but they were well capable of checking the antenna systems—which they had duly done, reporting back that everything was in order. But Ondray wanted to see for himself. *How could the Ship have lost contact with both Earth and Mars?* He also wanted to exert his authority. He wasn't going to stay inside the Ship just because some damned machine intelligence—two bloody machine intelligences—told him to. Sure, let the Protector protect him, and let Link advise; but *he* decided where, and when, he would go.

He caught a flash of light off to one side, and frowned. Then, he saw what it was that had caught his eye. Carefully turning his head, he looked out the other way. Sure enough, two of the long- legged machines were keeping tabs on him, close enough to hustle him back in to the airlock at the first sign of trouble, not so close as to get in his way.

The Protector being ultra protective?, Ondray wondered. *A watchdog and a backup? Or more probably one each—one surrogate for the Protector and one for Link himself.* It was, in spite of their recent differences of opinion, nice to know that they did, in their own way, care about what happened to him. He smiled to himself, shaking his head inside the helmet. Well, the three of them were well and truly stuck with each other, now.

Better get on with the job. Of course, the antennas would be in perfect working order. Of course, the breakdown of communications had been at the Earth end of the link. But he had to *know*; see for himself, feel with his own hands, as far as possible inside the bright yellow suit.

And he had to think, before he went back inside the Ship. Think very carefully about just how all this affected the balance of power within the Ship. Whatever had happened back home, they *had* to complete the mission, and stop the disturbance in the comet belt. But how best to persuade the Protector, in particular, that this did not involve unnecessary risk? Unnecessary risk to the body that might, the Protector kept insisting, represent the last human being there was to protect.

Twenty-one

ONDRAY WAS RESTING, HALF DOZING, WHEN HE WAS ROUSED by a sudden drumming on the roof of the rover. The vehicle was on auto, picking its way at a good speed around the stalagmite-like spires of rock along the route they had so painfully pioneered the previous day, with Tolly at the controls as backup. It was still dark; but as Ondray stood he could see over Tolly's shoulder, in the light of the headlights, white lumps, the size of large peas, falling from the sky, bouncing high in the low gravity, and settling back to cover the ground. Hail! Hail, on Mars.

The dark sky was suddenly lit by a sheet of blue-white light, showing the white covering stretching far beyond the range of the lights; then it was dark again. The accompanying crack of thunder was ridiculously feeble by terrestrial standards, sounding distant to ears that had grown up on Earth, but obviously right on top of them, since the sound followed hard on the heels of the flash. It seemed to have struck something just in front of them, to the left.

He pushed through, past Tolly, to the left hand seat. As he did so, Tolly turned to speak. The rover carried on, its moronic autopilot taking no notice of the change in the conditions outside, still steering over its programmed route, using the profusion of landmarks provided by the rocky spires.

Ondray was half in, half out of his seat, not listening to what Tolly had started to say, when everything fell apart. A pillar of rock to the left began to tilt towards them, agonisingly slowly. Red lights flashed on the panel, and as the autopilot set the brakes at emergency Tolly and Ondray both reached for the override, knocking each other out of the way as they did so. With wheels locked, the rover slid sideways on the icy surface, coming to a none-too-gentle halt against the stump of the fallen rock spire. Then, as the trailer behind tried to overtake them, they were jerked backwards and to the left, with the rover-trailer combination jackknifed around the rock stump.

Ondray's head banged hard against the bubble of clear plastic above the control panel, and he fell back, stunned, into his seat. The lights were pointing slightly up into the sky, and as he sat there, dazed, he could see the white lumps of hail changing to large drops of rain, falling gently through the white beams of light. Falling to turn the dust beneath the rover into mud—mud that would begin to freeze solid once the rain stopped.

Twenty-two

ONDRAY PUNCHED THE PAD TO OPEN THE INNER AIRLOCK door. Even floating free inside the airlock, gripping a hand-hold with his left hand, he felt tired. There was, of course, nothing wrong with the antenna systems. And Link assured him there was nothing wrong with the communications circuits. The problem must be on Earth. Their mission really might be a waste of time; they might already be too late.

But what choice did they have but to go on? He felt close to tears, but the logical part of his mind was still functioning well enough to tell him that this wasn't entirely because of the breakdown of communications. This bloody organic body was also a waste of time; the tiniest bit of exertion and he was too exhausted to think straight. At least he could do something about that.

Don't start the rotation of the Ship yet, Link.

At least he wouldn't have to suffer gravity for a while yet. It was, of course, the nagging nursemaid of the Protector who responded.

GRAVITY IS IMPORTANT FOR THE FUNCTIONING OF THE HUMAN BODY.

It was as if the Protector was reading his thoughts. Perhaps he was—Ondray was never quite sure how much leaked out through this net, even when it was supposed to be private.

It won't hurt to be in free fall a little longer. He wondered whether his anger seeped through as well. Hope so. Might blow a few circuits and make that bloody Protector a bit less solemn. He pulled himself along the gently spiraling corridor; the airlock was one of three grouped symmetrically around the nose of the Ship, and the winding corridor took him just inside the skin of the vessel, out and down to the hibernation units, housed where the curving nose had flared out to the full diameter of the main cylindrical body of the craft. Where they could receive full benefit of the pseudo gravity caused by rotation.

He knew that the Protector was right. And Link, by his silence, was implicitly reinforcing the Protector, on this occasion. His human body had to be kept in a gravity field, or the equivalent, for its long term well being. Right now, it also needed sleep. But there was no way Ondray intended to be out of touch with what was going on, as long as the Ship was out of touch with the rest of humankind. And there was no way he was going to be trying to cope with dulled senses, when he would need all his wits about him in order to make sure that Link and the Protector followed the right course of action.

I'm going back to the hibernation pod, where the body will be safe.

Excellent. I'm sure that is wise.

THE HUMAN MUST BE PROTECTED.

So you agree that the safest place for this body is in the hibernation pod?

YES.

But our mission is still very important.

THERE MAY NOT BE ANY HUMANS LEFT ON EARTH TO HELP. Or on Mars, Ondray thought to himself, quickly suppressing the image of Tugela that floated, unbidden, into his mind.

We don't know that. If there are humans still alive on Earth, and they are in trouble, our mission is even more important. We must do what we can to stabilise the comet belt and help them.

MY PRIME DIRECTIVE IS TO PROTECT HUMANS. IF YOU ARE THE LAST HUMAN, I CANNOT TAKE ANY RISKS WITH YOUR BODY.

At last Link intervened. *But there is a good probability that other humans need your help as well. You must protect this body, but still take reasonable risks to help them.*

THE SITUATION IS UNCLEAR. IF THE SITUATION IS UNCLEAR, THE PRIME DIRECTIVE IS OF OVERRIDING IMPORTANCE.

But we must both obey the orders of a competent adult human.

PROVIDED THOSE ORDERS DO NOT CONFLICT WITH THE PRIME DIRECTIVE.

Link had given Ondray the opening he needed, just as he arrived at the entrance to the new hibernation unit.

Then my orders are simple. Put this body back into hibernation, and protect it carefully. Start up the spin again so that it has the right weight. Continue with the mission as long as there is no clear and immediate danger to the body. I will rejoin you, and together we will try to solve the problem of the breakdown of communications with Earth.

ORDERS MUST BE OBEYED.

Even through the net, Ondray could tell that the Protector was unhappy. But the direct order, and the lack of a direct threat to the body, would, surely, have set up a potential in the circuits strongly enough in his favour. If his status as possibly the last human made his life more important, it also, surely, meant that his orders carried more weight. And once he was back in the circuits himself, he could find more subtle ways to keep control of the systems out of the Protector's influence. But there was one more thing to check.

This order must still be obeyed even when the body is in hibernation.

AS LONG AS THE BODY LIVES. AND AS LONG AS THERE IS NO DIRECT THREAT TO THE HUMAN.

It would have to do. The Protector clearly recognised that even in hibernation the body's authority still carried weight. And between them, Link and he could surely influence the definition of what a "direct threat" might be, when they eventually got out to the comet belt and found out what was going on.

The pod, open in front of him, looked inviting. Tiredly, he stripped off the spacesuit, leaving it floating in the chamber. The robots, clinging to the wall and watching him, could deal with it later.

He pulled himself over to the pod and inside, swinging himself onto his back and holding both edges with his hands to stop the body bouncing out again.

OK, Link. Start the rotation again. And tell your helpers here to get on with putting this body to sleep. I'm ready to transfer when you are.

Twenty-three

THE INTENSE BURST OF RAIN WAS ALREADY FADING AWAY BY the time Ondray finished being sick. Tolly had been quick to come to his assistance, helping him out of the seat and onto the bunk at the rear of the vehicle; but his head still hurt, and he had just about emptied the contents of his stomach onto the floor. But he was sufficiently aware of his surroundings to notice at once that the sound of rain on the roof had stopped.

"Leave it," he murmured.

Tolly had already cleaned up the bulk of the vomit, dumping it into the recycler; now he had returned and was kneeling, with a pad of cleanser from the toilet, working at the remaining stain. He looked up as Ondray first swung his feet off the bunk, and then raised his right hand to his head, trying to hold it still and stop the dizziness.

"The rain's stopped. It doesn't matter what it smells like in here. We've got to get the trailer straightened out. Get on the move."

Tolly smiled. Even kneeling, his head was about level with Ondray's as Ondray sat, half leaning forward, on the bunk. He reached out and put a hand on Ondray's shoulder.

"You mean *I'd* better get out and straighten up the trailer. You're in no state. Besides, I'll need someone in here to juggle the rover to and fro."

There was no point in arguing. Tolly was right—somebody had to manouver the rover, and somebody else had to attend to unhitching and re-hitching the trailer. And the somebody outside, in the full suit, probably ought not to be the one who felt like throwing up.

He began to nod, then stopped as the motion of his head sent renewed waves of nausea through his body.

Tolly leaned forward, anxiously.

"How bad is it? You hit your head pretty hard."

Ondray grunted.

"Let me see your eyes."

He lifted his head slightly, opened his eyes wide. Tolly peered intently at them.

"The left pupil seems to be a bit dilated, Ondray. You may have concussion."

"So what? The people at Terranova can't wait. I'll just have to do the best I can."

"Yeah." Tolly stood, moved towards the control panel.

"Where're you goin'?"

"Thought I'd better tell then what's going on."

"No!" Ondray put as much strength as he could into the word, stopping Tolly in his tracks.

"There's no point, Tolly. No need to worry them. We'll get this thing back on the road, *then* call them with a new schedule. They can't do anything to help. Any more bad news might cause panic. Don't make it harder for Hoffa to keep things under control."

"I guess." Tolly sounded doubtful, but he showed no sign of going against Ondray's wishes. "Better suit up, then."

∎

Sitting in the left hand command seat again—this time properly strapped in—Ondray felt better. At least, he told himself, he felt less bad. He didn't have to move his head much; all the controls were at hand, and he could watch what was going on outside on the screen, thanks to the rear-view camera.

Tolly had carefully charged the oxygen pack in his green suit from the rover's tanks before cycling through the airlock and out onto the strangely altered surface. Instead of sending up puffs of dust as he walked, his feet seemed to stick, as if he was walking on a surface coated with honey. But soon, the water in the fresh mud would freeze. Or would it sublimate? Ondray wasn't sure, and right now he didn't really care. Whatever happened to the water they had to get out of here and get help to the colonists at Terranova.

He ran a systems check while Tolly was inspecting the problem outside and preparing to unhitch the trailer.

There was plenty of power; enough water to take a bath in; more than enough food for a week, the way he felt now. The limiting factor was oxygen.

After they'd picked up the trailer, they'd had enough for about 45 hours for the two of them. They'd been about 24 hours out from Terranova, under normal conditions; certainly no more than 30 hours even allowing for the detour through the pillared terrain. Six hours on the road before the accident, an hour spent getting sorted out since then, and a full four hour charge in Tolly's pack (equivalent to two hours' oxygen for the pair of them, of course)and they still had 36 hours oxygen for a journey that might take 24 hours, 25 at worst. And at that, Tolly wasn't going to use up all the oxygen in his suit.

It wasn't exactly a comfortable safety margin. Nothing he'd condone in normal circumstances. But it was enough—and these certainly were not normal circumstances.

The green figure on the screen, lit by the rover's spotlights, waved an arm above its head. His voice came over on the circuit.

"Ready to unhitch, Tolly."

"OK. How shall I take it?"

"Swing round to your right, then back up. The trailer's wedged against the pillar, but no real damage, just the skin bent a little. If you pull out slowly heading about 20 degrees right, it should come clear. Then you'll have to pick out a wider circle through the best part of 360 degrees to get back on track. It'll have to be at walking pace, though. I'll stay out here and guide you through the pillars."

"OK."

He watched the green-suited figure working at the connecting link. It should have come unhitched immediately, but something seemed to be wrong. The figure stood upright again, waving both his hands across his knees to signify failure.

"It's stuck. Still in tension, and at a weird angle. There's a slight downslope," he gestured to show that the ground sloped away past the pillar, from the angle of the "V" made by the jack-knifed combination, "so the weight of the rover is still pulling on the link. You'll have to back up a tiny touch to release the tension. Then it should be OK."

"No problem."

Tolly moved to the right of the rear-view screen, between the rover and the pillar of rock that the trailer was jammed against from the other side. He was safely out of the way of the rover's intended movements as Ondray engaged reverse and gently nudged the vehicle backwards. But at the first touch of movement, the whole combination suddenly lurched to his left as the pressure that had been holding the trailer pressed against the rock pillar eased. The trailer scraped against the pillar, dragging the rover itself sideways down the slight incline and bringing it up hard against the base of the rock.

Under Mars gravity, even on a slippery incline the vehicle didn't gather much speed in the few feet to the pillar, and the impact was slight. Tolly had ample time to move out of the way, but as he did so he slipped on the now icy surface himself, and fell to the ground.

The pillar had already been cracked in the original impact. Now, hit another blow from a different direction, a piece of rock like the trunk of a small tree, twice as tall as Ondray and about as thick around the middle as Tolly fell from the spire. The camera, tracking Tolly's efforts to get to his feet, saw nothing until it was too late; Tolly, on all fours, head down as he regained a grip on the surface, saw nothing at all as the end of the falling rock smashed across his hips and lower back, crushing him to the ground. There was no sound. Ondray stared at the screen for long seconds before he could move.

"Tolly?"

There was no reply.

Automatically, he was unfastening his safety harness and out of the seat. His head still hurt, and his brain reported symptoms of nausea, down at some level in the body. But these problems no longer seemed to matter. On a surge of adrenaline, Ondray suited up, quickly but carefully, making sure that his suit was charged with a full four-hour breathing supply. No point in getting out there 40 seconds quicker but with the suit not properly sealed. No point in running out of oxygen halfway through the job.

Outside, it was quiet and still. Tolly lay, unmoving under the finger of rock in the pool of illumination from the rover's lights. The ground was still slippery, but it was quite easy to move carefully over to his side, where Ondray knelt to inspect the damage.

It didn't look good. They were almost exactly halfway between Terranova and New Tycho, where the few autosurgeries that the colonists had been permitted to bring from Earth had to be kept, for the benefit of the bulk of the population. And Tolly must surely have suffered broken bones in the hip and pelvis area.

At least the integrity of his suit didn't seem to have suffered. It was still ballooned out around his upper body and legs, even though it was pressed flat against his hips by the weight of the rock finger. But Ondray was forced to correct this first impression almost as he reached it. The suit was still pressurised, all right; but a cautious prod with his gloved finger at the fabric over Tolly's upper body showed that it wasn't fully pressurised. There must be damage, underneath the rock, with oxygen-enriched air leaking out of the suit.

The suit's automatic systems would compensate as best they could, raising the pressure to make up for the leakage. But that meant the oxygen would be used up more quickly.

Ondray chinned the pad in his helmet for a time display, which flashed up on the clear visor in front of his eyes. It was nearly 90 minutes since Tolly had left the rover. So he had about two and a half hours of oxygen at best, less whatever was leaking away.

Ondray lay flat on the ground, carefully avoiding touching the rock or Tolly, shining his helmet light underneath the rock to check the damage. He could see very little, and in any case his options were limited. He had to get the rock off Tolly, and Tolly back into the rover, double quick—even at the risk of doing more damage to his abdomen.

There was a jack in the toolkit at the rear of the rover. It ought to be sufficient to lift the rock, but he'd have to take care it didn't topple. And there was a simple stretcher—

nothing like as sophisticated as a full surgery, but it could lift the patient and provide basic painkillers.

Ondray squatted on his haunches for a few minutes, thinking it through. If he could get everything in one trip back to the rover he would avoid wasting time later on. And if moving the rock allowed even more air to escape from Tolly's suit, as he feared it might, he'd better have absolutely everything on hand after he started lifting.

Tolly's left hand moved slightly, feebly scraping at the ground. Ondray heard something over the audio link—no words, just an animal-like moan of pain.

"Don't move, Tolly." The scrabbling, and the noise, stopped. "Don't try to speak. You're pinned down by a rock. I'm going to move it and get you back inside. All you have to do is lie still."

"How. Bad. Is. It?" The words were hissed out, one by one, obviously through clenched teeth. Tolly was a loonie; he would want to know the truth.

"It's bad, Tolly. Don't try to move at all."

There was only a grunt in response.

Ondray stood, and moved carefully but quickly back to the rover. The ground was no longer so slippery; some of the ice seemed to have disappeared. Part of his brain wondered at the weird hydrological cycle that seemed to be becoming established, with water falling from the sky and freezing before sublimating back into vapour. But even while he was musing on the strange phenomenon, he was efficiently gathering the tools he needed and piling them on to the stretcher for the short journey back over to Tolly.

Even with the weight of the jack on it, and everything else, the stretcher still floated a comfortable metre above the ground. Ancient Earth technology, operating under Mars gravity. At least it made part of his job easier, although he still found he was sweating inside the suit, and panting with the exertion of manouvering the heavy objects.

He wasn't sure if Tolly had slipped into unconsciousness again, or was simply obeying Ondray's instructions and keeping quiet. Well, there was nothing for him to do, and conversation would only distract Ondray.

He placed the jack carefully under the end of the rock finger jutting out past Tolly's back, and brought it up into contact with the underside of the rock. The stretcher, lift off, lay as close as possible to Tolly's body, between Tolly and the jack; he only needed to lift the jack a foot or so and he could roll Tolly straight onto the stretcher. He checked the other end of the rock finger, resting on the ground on the other side of Tolly's body. On one side, it was securely wedged, jammed against some ancient boulders. He piled rocks around the other side of the stump. Surely it wouldn't shift in the minute or so he would need.

As he chinned the pad to check the time again, Ondray noticed sweat dripping into his eyes, making it hard to read the display. Another 45 minutes gone; surely that couldn't be right? But he certainly felt as sore as if he'd been hauling tools and rocks around for well over half an hour.

"Can you hear me, Tolly?"

A grunt.

"I'm going to lift the rock, roll you on to the stretcher, and get you inside. It's going to hurt." "All. Ready. Bloody. Hurts."

"Yeah. Don't try to talk. Can you chin the emergency oxygen boost?"

Idiot. Telling him not to talk then asking a question!

"O. K."

He couldn't see the head movement inside the helmet, but suddenly Tolly's flabby suit began to take on a more solid appearance. Increased pressure would almost certainly blow any weak patches once the rock lifted, but if they blew without the increased pressure Tolly wouldn't stand a chance.

Time to move, and quickly.

The jack was already set to give him eighteen inches of lift. He stabbed at the button, and as the piston smoothly lifted the rock away from Tolly's body he shoved the stretcher right alongside him, reaching across to roll the body, in one swift movement, over on to it. As he did so, he saw a torn piece of suit fabric flapping as air escaped from it; but at least the damaged area was now underneath Tolly as he lay on his back on the stretcher.

One cry of pain had escaped from his lips as Ondray had to roll him over; but through the visor Ondray could see that his eyes were now shut, head lolling to one side. He'd passed out again—probably the best thing that could have happened.

There wasn't enough clearance to lift the stretcher until Ondray had crawled out from under the balanced rock finger and dragged the stretcher forward; then, he was up, the stretcher was on full lift, and they were headed back into the ready-open airlock. Inside, he secured the stretcher and cut Tolly's suit away from his upper body, after gently removing the helmet. He didn't dare investigate the damage below Tolly's waist. Once Tolly's left arm was bare, Ondray laid it gently in the groove at the side of the stretcher, where the systems could administer their limited medication. He punched the code for painkillers; there wasn't much else he could do, now, except get them back to Terranova, soonest. And that meant finishing the job of re-hitching the trailer and manouvering the rig out of this mess.

First, he had to go outside and complete the unhitching. The jack and pile of tools caught his eye; he was tempted to leave them. But what if they had another accident? And who would ever take his orders seriously again if he was seen to disregard them himself whenever there was a little local difficulty? Muttering to himself about his aches and pains, Ondray got everything stowed.

Then, back into the vehicle, jiggling it around as Tolly had suggested, backing up at the right angle to haul the trailer clear of the rock spire. The sweat was fogging his visor by now, and it was hard to see the rear view screen clearly enough to get the connecting link locked in place, but he made it at the third attempt.

Back out again to secure the link and double-check his planned grand circle out and round the pillars and back on to the known route through the pillared terrain. *And then,* Ondray told himself as he stood, leaning with one hand on the side of the rover, getting his bearings clear, *put the beast on autopilot, get out of this suit, take a shower.*

It was at that moment that the oxygen warning light began to flash its insistent red signal in the corner of his field of vision.

Already? he thought, as he checked the time display. He'd suited up less than three hours ago, but the display said 15 minutes oxygen left. Fifteen minutes at normal exertion, that was; at the rate he'd been going, it probably wouldn't last ten. He'd finished everything just in time—and it was even beginning to get light.

But it wasn't light enough to make driving easy, especially for someone as tired as Ondray now was. Helmetless, but still otherwise suited up, he sat at the controls, picking his way carefully around one pillar after another, until his eyes felt as if they were scratching the inside of his head and his tongue was like a piece of fur in his mouth. Twice he thought they had regained the known route, but each time the autopilot rejected it. It was when he was careless enough to brush the left of the rover against a rock pillar, sending an echoing boom through the cabin, that he realised he simply had to stop for a few minutes, to drink, and take that long promised shower. Sleep would have to wait until the autopilot said it was happy with the route.

Tolly's eyes were open as Ondray returned to the rear of the vehicle.

"Hey! You're awake."

His face was completely drained of colour; even his lips looked white. But Tolly managed a thin smile. "Your lousy driving; enough to wake anybody."

"Yeah. Sorry about that. I'm just going to freshen up."

"Sorry I can't help."

Ondray waved his right hand in a dismissive gesture.

"No problem. I just need a drink and some stimtabs. How do you feel?"

"I don't. Not a thing."

They were both silent for a moment.

"That's bad, isn't it?"

"Not good. But the surgery in Terranova will fix you up."

"Yeah."

If, Ondray thought, *you last that long.* But he just smiled, and stripped off his suit. A drink followed by a quick shower made him feel better; the stimtabs made him positively bright eyed. He knew he'd pay the price for his alertness later, but right now he felt great; really in command of the situation. Should have thought of this sooner, then he wouldn't have been so messy, dumping his suit here in the main cabin, instead of changing in the airlock and vacuuming up all the dust. It really was filthy in here.

He was on his way to check Tolly's condition when he paused.

All this filth—it hadn't come from one suit. Not even from Tolly's suit. Of course, when he'd been dashing in and out he hadn't been going through the standard procedure.

How many exits and entrances had he made? He couldn't remember, but it must have been about half a dozen. Using the emergency override each time, and dumping a lock full of breathable air out into the Martian atmosphere each time. Trailing dust everywhere. Even, he realised, leaving the inner airlock door open on the last occasion.

He went over to shut it, and noticed the way the dust had piled up around the seal of the outer door. That was strange. He knelt to take a look. Some of the dust grains seemed to be moving towards the door.

Suddenly cold, Ondray licked a finger and held it to the seal. Barely discernable, but definitely there, he felt the cool whisper of a breeze.

The lock wasn't airtight!

He quickly grabbed the vacuum hose, and worked his way thoroughly around the seal of the inner door, before retreating back inside the main cabin and securing the door. Another licked finger, held to the seal, revealed no trace of a draught. The rover was airtight again.

But how much air had they lost?

He turned back towards the controls, trying to work it out in his head. They'd had about 37 hours of air when Tolly was crushed. He'd used a suit full, and the rest of the air in Tolly's suit had gone, which took it down to, what, 34? 33? Then the loss through the airlock with all his comings and goings—not enough to worry about, usually. An hour at most. They'd been three hours on the road since. Should be about 28, 29 hours left. And they couldn't be much more than 20 hours from Terranova, surely.

He looked at the display. He'd scarcely glanced at it since they had got on the move again, peering intently out, first into the semi-darkness, and then across the long interlaced shadows of the pillars as the Sun had risen clear of the horizon. The display was quite clear, designed to be unambiguous for any idiot driving around on the Martian surface.

Air remaining at present rate of consumption, it said.

And underneath, in large, black letters:

17 HOURS 47 MINUTES.

As he watched, the "47" was replaced by a "46". Less than 18 hours air for a 20 hour journey. For two people.

There really wasn't any choice.

He stood up, slowly, and went back to check Tolly's condition. He was asleep, or unconscious, still looking like death, but breathing, shallowly. *Would he last 20 hours, anyway?* He might, of course, have been killed by the falling rock. Then there'd have been no problem. Not that there really was a problem; thousands of lives at Terranova depended on the supplies in the trailer getting through. One life, more or less, weighed little in the opposite pan of the balance.

Ondray went back to the controls, started the rover moving forward. It was easier to drive, now that the Sun was higher in the sky and the shadows were shorter. And, of course, now that it was too late to make a difference, he found the right road almost immediately. They weren't far from the spot where he'd seen that one lone plant—it seemed like half a lifetime ago, but it must have been only the day before yesterday. As good a place as any.

He checked with the autopilot. Yes, the idiot machine was quite happy. It knew the way back to Terranova from here.

Good.

Once again, he brought the vehicle to a halt, went back to the airlock, and climbed into the yellow suit. It stank of sweat, but he knew from experience that his nostrils would ignore the odour once he was sealed in.

Before attaching the helmet, he checked round the cabin, tidying it as much as he could. As an afterthought, with the inner airlock door open again he used the vacuum line to clean the dust off the floor and all the other surfaces it had crept onto. It wouldn't be good for his authority for the vehicle to arrive at Terranova in a filthy state.

He looked around again, touched Tolly's right hand.

Tolly had meant well; and he'd certainly learnt his lesson.

He went forward to the control panel, punched a sequence of coded instructions into the console. Ten minutes would do.

At last, Ondray attached the helmet. The red light was still flashing; but 15 minutes air would be ample for what he had in mind. Carefully sealing the inner door behind him, he passed through the airlock and out onto the surface of Mars.

The slump of the mud slide that had swamped his lone wild plant was a few minutes walk away. He set out towards it at a brisk pace. Behind him, as the ten minutes set on the timer elapsed, the rover started moving again, down the track towards Terranova. But there was no point in turning around to watch. He chinned the bar to start the suit recorder running, and began to talk as he strode towards the hillock.

I can sit up there, he thought, *and admire the view. For the rest of my life.*

"Hello, Tugela," he began. "I want to tell you about something I found out here, a couple of days ago . . ."

Twenty-four

CLEARING THE PHYSICAL DAMAGE IN THE VILLAGES NEAR R'apehu, and rehousing the villagers, took time and effort. Neither could easily be spared, since the really important work of restoration had to go on in the fields—fields where the crops had been suffering for decades in the cooling climate.

The farmers had adapted, as best they could. Crops from further south had been introduced in this northern island, and thrived, for a time. But in the wake of the comet the weather seemed even cooler, and distinctly wetter, than it had been. Perhaps the comet impact had helped to tip the climatic balance, after decades of slow decline, into a new pattern.

Anxious studies were made of the records suggesting a link between the changing pattern of solar activity and the declining climate. Perhaps, it was argued, the rebuilding of the R'apehu observatory ought to be given a higher priority, after all—not because there seemed to be any urgent need to re-establish the communications link with the Ship, let alone Mars. Because it might, after all, be invaluable in its original role, as an astronomical observatory. There might be nothing they could do to reverse the change in climate;

but even having some knowledge of what might be in store next year, or next decade, would help in their agricultural planning.

Twenty-five

IT WAS DAWN AGAIN, BEGINNING TO GET LIGHTER, WHEN THE
rover appeared over the gentle ridge on the road outside
Terranova, its lights bright on the horizon. Inside, Tolly lay
unmoving, eyes closed, on the stretcher; the trailer bounced
along safely in the wake of the vehicle.

For half a day, both Terranova and New Tycho had been
trying, with increasing urgency and alarm, to make contact
with the occupants of the rover. But the machine simply
was not intelligent enough to indulge in conversation. All
that the interrogators received in response was the "Here I
Am" beacon, telling them of the steady progress of the relief
supplies towards their intended destination.

Now, the rover had arrived. Happily, the idiot brain of
the machine brought it to a halt the statutory hundred
metres from the main entrance, and sent the signal
requesting human assistance. There was no need for this;
suited figures had been waiting outside for the supplies
even before the rig had crested the ridge. But the programming said that the rig had to be brought to a halt a hundred
metres out, and human assistance had to be requested.
So it was, even though human figures were scurrying all
around the rig.

■

Some 20 hours drive away down the track to New Tycho, there was a suited figure that wasn't doing any scurrying. It was sitting, motionless, back against a large boulder. Curiously, though, the figure wasn't sitting on the top of the mud slide, which would have provided the best view of the surroundings. It was nearer to the bottom of the hillock than the top.

When people came back along the track, as they would as soon as the rover had been serviced and turned around, the yellow figure would be obvious, even from a distance. When they approached, the face behind the visor would seem to be asleep, eyes closed, something like a smile frozen on its lips. But it would be easy to see where the eyes would look, if they happened to open again.

Of course, the figure's head might have tilted forward, as the body slipped into unconsciousness and the eyes closed for the last time. But if the figure had been sitting exactly as it would be found, but with eyes open, then Ondray's last view would not have been of the distant horizon and the harsh Martian scenery, after all. Instead, his gaze seemed to be focused on a crack in the surface of the frozen mud, a crack probably caused by frost, about two metres in front of his body. A crack in which a tiny tendril could just be discerned, reaching upward for the sunlight.

Twenty-six

TEN TIMES FURTHER OUT FROM THE SUN THAN JUPITER, fifty times further out than the orbit of the Earth, and four times as far beyond the orbit of Neptune as the distance of Jupiter from the Sun, the Sun itself appeared as no more than a bright star to the sensors on board the Ship, unless they used magnification. The light which fell on those sensors had taken just under nine hours to travel across the void on its outward journey into space; the signals that the Ship still beamed back towards Earth and Mars would take just as long to arrive at their intended destinations. But it was now more than a year, by Earth calendars, since any signal from either planet had reached the Ship.

The shared intelligence of the Ship, the entity that had once been the separate intelligences of Ondray, Link and Lagrange, had no way of knowing if any human life remained on either planet. But the imperative built in to two-thirds of that intelligence, and Ondray's freely derived sense of duty, gave it no choice. They had to find the reason for the disturbance in the cometary cloud, and restore things to normal. Only then could there be any hope of stabilising conditions in the inner Solar System, and allowing both branches of the human species a chance to recover from whatever catastrophes had befallen them.

At least there was a chance of dealing with a disturbance this close to the Sun. Distant though they were from the inner Solar System, the main spherical shell of comets that surrounded the Sun still lay a thousand times further out into space, almost halfway to the nearer stars, so far from the Sun that it took light more than a year to make the journey out and past them.

Disturbed by the changing gravitational forces of the nearby stars, comets from the outer cloud were constantly feeding inwards, over the eons, interacting with one another and with the gravitational tug of the outer planets of the Solar System to form a great disc around the Sun, like the ring system around Saturn but on a far grander scale, extending from a little beyond the orbit of Neptune out to a thousand times the distance of the Earth from the Sun, and containing roughly a hundred million comets. The outer regions of this disc were constantly being replenished by new arrivals from the outer cloud, while repeated interactions within the disc set comets drifting inward, eventually to be torn away from the inner edge of the disc by the gravitational tug of the outer planets, and sent falling inward on trajectories that would carry many of them within the orbit of Jupiter, to blaze briefly across the skies of the inner Solar System. Just a few of these comets ought to be being herded by the two *Perseus* craft into orbits that would actually intersect the orbit of Mars, carrying their burden of water and other volatile materials to help the terraforming of the red planet.

But all that had changed. The total mass of all the comets in this vast disc was only a few times the mass of the Earth, and any large enough mass, passing through the disc and settling in to an orbit within the disc, would inevitably spread a gravitational disturbance outward from its path, tumbling scores of comets free from their orbits and sending some inward towards the Sun, while others climbed out again, back towards the cloud in which they had originated. The same effect had been achieved by the passage of a vessel whose engines manipulated the fabric of spacetime itself, gripping space in a pseudo-gravitational grip in order to thrust itself forward.

Observations of the orbits of infalling comets from the Earth and the Moon, supplemented by data from the *Perseus* craft, had shown roughly where in the ring the intruding mass was orbiting; with the observations refined by the Ship's own instruments as it had moved out past Jupiter, the trajectory of the vessel had been fine tuned to bring it close to the site of the disturbance. Close enough for the gravitational anomaly and its effects to be felt and tasted by the intelligence on board the Ship, using the variety of sensors linked to their mind.

The part of the mind that was Ondray still felt the input in human terms. Stars were visible, as points of light. There was the patter of occasional cosmic ray particles, like a light shower of rain, and the faint hiss of white noise in the channel kept constantly open on the communications receiver kept permanently pointed at Mars. The anomaly was like a whirlpool, swirling unseen in the void, but dragging spacetime around, constantly edging the Ship off course. The effect was small, but to the machine senses of the intelligence on board the Ship, it was like swimming in a not quite still river, always having to paddle gently against the stream in order to stay in the same place. Sensors on board the Ship, and those carried by two spidery robots now flying in formation, one on either side of the Ship, each maintaining a distance of 100 kilometers, combined to pinpoint the position of the anomaly. But optical sensors showed nothing at all in that location. There was mass—large amounts of mass—but it was invisible.

Shifting the data on the gravitational anomaly into another channel, Ondray could perceive it as a coloured ball, pale blue against the blackness of space, moving slowly past a large cometary nucleus, several tens of kilometers across, that tumbled like a huge iceberg in its orbit around the Sun.

But there was something peculiar about the comet itself. As the intelligence watched, occasional jets of gas seemed to be emitted from the iceberg; the whole thing was surrounded by a tenuous cloud of gas, revealed by the way it absorbed the light from distant stars at the characteristic spectral wavelengths of water, ammonia, carbon dioxide and methane.

This far from the Sun, the iceberg should be utterly cold, frozen and inert. Energy for outgassing could come only if it floated in, past Jupiter, and warmed in the heat of the Sun. Where was the energy source responsible for all this activity?

Drifting in towards the iceberg/anomaly pair, the intelligence saw a chunk of ice suddenly break free from the mass, and move slowly outward, flung away by centrifugal force into its own orbit, an orbit curving unnaturally away from the comet nucleus under the influence of the anomaly. The part of the intelligence that was Ondray disengaged itself slightly from the joint mind. They found that this still made it easier to make plans, or to interpret new puzzles. Two "heads" were still better than one when it came to tossing new ideas back and forth and knocking them into shape.

The third head, Lagrange, still declined to volunteer anything to such a debate, although it would provide information when asked. The difficulty was knowing what to ask of the melding of computer intelligence, the human Planner who had helped design the original Ship, and the minds of the six loonies who had found their way to the Ship before the reunion.

Telescope, Link.

The suggestion was unnecessary, but it helped Ondray to establish his sense of individual identity again. He was, after all, a human being. The Link was merely a machine, albeit a rather special machine, and it was humans who gave orders, while machines, no matter how special, obeyed them.

It was like having a zoom control on your eyes. The fragment of comet suddenly seemed to leap towards them, enlarging to fill Ondray's field of vision. The definition wasn't perfect; after all, they were still several thousand kilometers from the anomaly. But it was good enough.

The comet fragment was perhaps twice as big as the Ship—a little shorter, but rather fatter. As it rotated, its irregular surface flashed in the faint light from the distant Sun, twinkling imperceptibly to human eyes, but like a beacon to the Ship's sensors.

One side of the chunk of ice, though, was not irregular. Completely flat, like a mirror surface, it was as smooth as if it had been cut away from the parent iceberg by a hot wire passing through the ice.

There was more. As they watched, a circular pit opened up in the ice. Starting in the centre of the flat face, boring right through the sliver and out the other side, to make as perfectly circular tunnel. But the ice being removed from the tunnel was not being spewed out into space behind whatever was boring its way through the interior. It simply disappeared, as if it had never been there.

A second tunnel, equally circular, equally mysterious, was bored out from the irregular face, back towards the flat face. At maximum magnification, the image jerking slightly as the sensors tracked the constantly changing position of the ice sliver relative to the Ship, they saw a circular hoop of light, a little greater in diameter than the Ship itself, appear for a moment out of the newly formed hole, highlighted against the dark surface of the ice. Then, it was gone from view, leaving the ice sliver, bored by two tunnels like some curious cosmic abstract sculpture, tumbling in its orbit past the anomaly.

Can we replay that, Link?

Of course. You spotted it too, then. Faster even than the exchange of "thoughts", Link had replayed the interesting segment of memory, and frozen it at the moment when the hoop of light had emerged from the new tunnel and lay directly in front of the ice sliver itself. The elliptical appearance of the hoop was, they knew from the wide angle vision provided by the outriding robot sensors, merely a trick of perspective; the hoop and both tunnels were really quite circular. The ice itself appeared blue-white in the image, enhanced from the few photons received by the sensors. Both tunnel mouths were in view, like circular black pits, looking out onto the darkness of space on the other side of the sliver. And there was a third black circle, just to the upper right of the new tunnel, edged by a red hoop of light.

If the disk were solid, as it seemed to be, that would explain why it blocked the reflected light from the ice behind. But if it were solid, it could only have created the tunnels through the ice by pushing a column of ice out ahead of itself as it forced its way through.

If the red circle was no more than a loop of something energetic—the equivalent of a hot wire—then it would be straightforward to understand how it could pass right through the ice sliver (and, indeed, how the sliver had been cut away so smoothly from the comet nucleus). But then, if it were no more than a hoop of energy, the cores of ice should have been left in place, still filling the tunnel. And if it were no more than a loop of energy, why didn't any light come through the hoop? *Not just no light, Ondray.* Of course, his thoughts were shared by Link; there was no real need to think them out loud.

No anything. Nothing at all, across the spectrum. It's as if the space inside that circle doesn't exist.

Like the anomaly.

Yes. Something that isn't there, doing something we don't understand. Taking bites out of something we do understand, and making the bitten off pieces disappear as well.

The conversation had merely been the surface flow on top of a current of data, analysing input from every sensor carried by the Ship and its robot attendants. The hoop showed, just barely, as a gravitational object, and it radiated weak electromagnetic radiation, in the radio band, which Ondray had been choosing to perceive as a red glow. But the disc it surrounded failed to register on any detector. It was blacker than space itself, with no cosmic rays, and no photons from the cosmic background radiation, let alone visible light, coming from its direction.

It looks like that thing is eating *the ice.*

Like a worm eating through an apple.

But surely it can't be alive?

Don't make any presumptions, Ondray. Rely on the data.

But the holes look rather regular for this to be a kind of space worm.

But where are the cores? They've been eaten out like they never existed.

Cores could be right, Ondray. Images of the core samples that the loonies had used on Mars to obtain samples from the polar caps flashed across Ondray's awareness. Both laser systems and mechanical drills, boring into the icy surface, extracting their long, cylindrical samples for analysis. The analysis that had showed the presence of enough water and carbon dioxide to add significantly to the atmosphere, if it could be thawed out by a covering of dark, heat absorbing algae. He remembered walking awkwardly across the ice, back to the landrover, directing the driver to come forward with the vehicle and collect the cores; Tugela's excitement at the news.

But none of that mattered. It was the cores themselves that mattered. *That hoop of light was behaving just like a core sampling drill back on Mars!*

Look at the anomaly.

Ondray turned his attention to the blue ball. It was moving, slowly, towards the bored-out ice sliver. It was clearly under power, not falling under the influence of gravity, although according to the Ship's sensors the mass of the anomaly had increased by 3.7 per cent as it had begun to move. Automatically, he created a routine to keep watch on the mass of the anomaly and report back any further changes.

Steadily, the blue ball drifted on a collision course towards the ice chunk. But instead of a collision, it simply engulfed the sliver.

Switching back to optical sensors, Ondray could see nothing except the ice sliver and the nearby cometary nucleus. And the sliver showed no sign of the impact.

Switching back to the false colour image of the gravitational anomaly, he watched the blue ball drift on, past the ice sliver, heading straight towards the comet nucleus itself. The edge of the ball brushed across the ice mountain, but neither the ball nor the comet took any notice—except, a nagging, pedantic monitor routine reminded him, for the slight change in the orbit of the comet caused by the gravitational influence of the anomaly. The new routine told him that the mass of the anomaly had decreased back to its previous value, and that it was no longer under power, but drifting in a long, slow orbit around the Sun with the rest of the material in the cometary disc.

If that loop had *been taking samples, Link . . .*

Then that would be just the behaviour you might expect if the anomaly was a parent ship going to pick them up.

Except that neither the anomaly nor the samples seem to exist.

Or they both *exist where we can't detect them.*

They needed more data. With both Earth and Mars incommunicado, that meant only one thing. As always, especially when he was partially separated from the group mind, Ondray was aware of the third component, away down in the memory banks of the old hibernation unit. If he "looked" directly for the Lagrange mind, he could see it as an orange ball, flecked with yellow and red. Even without looking, he was aware of it as something that his human-bred senses felt as a kind of growth at the base of his spine, like a second brain. Not that he had either a spine or a brain, when he was installed in the main memory with the Link. He existed everywhere, throughout the circuitry of the Ship—everywhere *except* in the old hibernation systems, jealously controlled by Lagrange.

The former Protector of the habitat that had become the Ship might be semi-autistic, but it still controlled access to data going back to the time when the habitat was built, and records installed into its memory of information from a previous era. Especially scientific records concerning the off-Earth environment. If humanity had ever contemplated the possible existence of anything as bizarre as that invisible warping of spacetime, Lagrange would have the information stored away, somewhere.

He directed a message at the orange ball.

Request analysis of gravitational anomaly.

As usual, instead of receiving an answer as a totality of information, a pooling of knowledge in the way that he pooled knowledge with Link, the response came back painfully slowly, a bit at a time, along the communications channel.

It was worse than reading incoming laser data from Earth. But the message spelled out by the trickle of bits was worth waiting for.

THE OBSERVATIONS ARE CONSISTENT WITH THE PRESENCE OF AN OBJECT COMPOSED OF MIRROR MATTER. PARTICLES OF MIRROR MATTER ARE REQUIRED BY THE STANDARD UNIFIED THEORY OF PHYSICS IN ORDER TO MAKE THE LAWS OF PHYSICS SYMMETRICAL. MIRROR PROTONS, NEUTRONS AND ELECTRONS SHOULD HAVE BEEN PRODUCED IN THE BIG BANG IN WHICH THE UNIVERSE WAS BORN, WITH ALL THEIR PROPERTIES, EXCEPT THEIR GRAVITATIONAL INTERACTION, REVERSED COMPARED WITH EVERYDAY MATTER. EVERYDAY MATTER AND MIRROR MATTER CAN INTERACT ONLY THROUGH GRAVITY. A MIRROR OBJECT COULD PASS RIGHT THROUGH AN ORDINARY OBJECT, SUCH AS THAT COMET OR OUR SHIP, WITHOUT EITHER BEING AFFECTED.

Ondray had only a vague awareness of ideas about the birth of the Universe, but while the message from Lagrange was spelling itself out, he had automatically tasted the Link's larger store of data on the subject. It made sense. If the Universe had been born in a high energy fireball, as all the evidence suggested, then the primordial energy flux should have broken down to form every kind of particle allowed by the laws of physics.

Without having to go through the arguments, from the totality of the package of information pooled to him by Link Ondray understood, at a gut level, the importance of symmetry in those laws, the requirement that every variety of left-handed particle must be balanced by a variety of right-handed particle. But the total *numbers* of each kind of particle need not be in balance.

How much mirror matter could there be?

IN ORDER TO WARP SPACETIME SUFFICIENTLY TO MAKE THE UNIVERSE CLOSED, THERE MUST BE AT LEAST TEN TIMES MORE DARK MATTER AROUND IN SOME FORM THAN THE AMOUNT OF MATTER WE SEE IN ALL THE BRIGHT STARS AND GALAZIES. THE SIMPLEST EXPLANATION IS THAT ALL OF THIS IS IN THE FORM OF MIRROR MATTER. *Ten times* as much mirror matter as ordinary matter? It seemed crazy.

Not necessarily crazy, Ondray. The evidence in favour of dark matter is overwhelming. There is no reason why the breaking of the original symmetry in the early Universe should have divided up the matter equally between the two varieties. We just happen to be made of minority stuff.

You mean there could be stars, and planets, and people, made of this stuff? Of course, he knew the answer, from the information being pooled by Link. But in this partially disengaged state, he was human enough to need time to think through the implications.

Stars, and planets, and people. And spacecraft. Almost certainly, an interstellar spacecraft, exploring what to them is the hidden tenth of the Universe.

Taking samples. And disturbing the comets by accident. But how—what is that loop? And how do we stop them?

The question hadn't been directed down the communications channel to Lagrange. But an answer came back along the channel anyway. It was the first time Ondray had known the former Protector to respond to a question that had not been specifically addressed to it. Maybe the impact of what they had found was shaking even Lagrange out of its autism.

THERE IS A FAINT POSSIBILITY THAT IT COULD BE A LOOP OF "ALICE STRING". THE SOURCE OF THE NOMENCLATURE IS UNCLEAR, BUT IT GOES BACK AT LEAST HALF A MILLE-NIUM. THE STRING WOULD BE A TUBE OF ENERGY LEFT OVER FROM THE BIG BANG ITSELF, A DEFECT IN THE STRUCTURE OF

SPACETIME. ANY OBJECT PASSING THROUGH AN ALICE LOOP WOULD BE CONVERTED INTO ITS MIRROR MATTER COUNTER-PART.

And when you pass back again?

THE THEORY IS UNCLEAR. ONE PASSAGE THROUGH SUCH A LOOP SHOULD HAVE NO HARMFUL EFFECT ON INORGANIC MATERIAL, BUT REVERSING THE PROCESS MAY NOT BE POSSIBLE.

What about organic material?

ALMOST CERTAINLY, ANY ATTEMPT TO CONVERT A LIVING OBJECT FROM ORDINARY MATTER INTO ALICE MATTER WILL RESULT IN DEATH. LIFE IS VERY COMPLEEX, ONDRAY, BOTH LEFT-HANDED AND RIGHT-HANDED FORMS ARE THEORETICALLY POSSIBLE, BUT NOT INTERCHANGE-ABLE. THE OBJECT WILL BE CONVERTED, BUT IT WILL NO LONGER BE ALIVE.

Lagrange had called him by name! Another first—but he was given no time to investigate the additional evidence of the mind's further step back from the borders of insanity.

You may soon have a chance to find out, Ondray.

He turned his attention back to the sensors that had been maintaining a watch over the anomaly/loop/comet complex. The image had scarcely changed; the entire "conversation" between himself, Link and Lagrange, even restricted to the pitifully slow pace of Lagrange's communications channel, had taken only a little over a second. But the ranging data from the two outlying probes showed that one of the components of the complex had altered its behaviour. The circular loop of Alice string, showing red against the black backdrop in the video channel, was moving, slowly but steadily, on an orbit that would intersect that of the Ship in just under twelve hours.

He scarcely noticed the trickle of a further message from the base of his spine up into his brain.

IN ANSWER TO YOUR SECOND QUESTION, ONE OF US WILL HAVE TO PASS THROUGH THE LOOP AND COMMUNICATE WITH THE MIRROR PEOPLE. HUMAN LIVES ARE AT STAKE.

If Lagrange is right, that thing could take a slice out of us as easily as it did the comet.

What we have to do is show them that we are intelligent—not a piece of cometary debris to be sampled.

Ondray tasted the flow of data. There was enough room—perhaps twenty meters to spare. *We could take the whole Ship through, in one piece.*

IT IS NECESSARY TO PRESERVE THE LIFE OF THE HUMAN.

Lagrange really was waking up—now it was offering unsolicited advice. But its timing was less than perfect. Tact was called for.

You said we had to go through, Protector. We have to communicate with the intelligence behind that thing. Make them go away, stop disturbing the comet cloud.

IT IS NECESSARY TO PRESERVE THE LIFE OF THE HUMAN.

What about the humans on Earth, and on Mars? We came all this way to help them. *It doesn't matter if the Ondray clone in hibernation doesn't survive; I'll still be here. We can always grow me another body, later, just as we did last time.* WE DO NOT KNOW THAT ANY LIFE REMAINS ON EARTH, OR ON MARS. WE MUST ACT AS IF IT DOES, AND REMOVE THE THREAT TO THAT LIFE. BUT THE ONDRAY CLONE MAY BE THE LAST HUMAN. IT IS MY DUTY TO PROTECT HUMAN LIFE.

Perhaps we can argue about this later, Ondray. The anomaly—the alien ship—is moving again.

He looked. The pale blue ball had increased in mass again, and was moving on a trajectory that would bring it alongside them in eight hours, twenty-seven minutes and 14.2 seconds, almost four hours before the Alice loop passed through the Ship—unless the Ship moved into a different orbit.

Thoughts raced through Ondray's mind. As each idea occurred to him, it was compared against the available data. Plans were rejected, only half-formed, as the information from all over the Ship, available at the speed of light, showed that it would be impossible to carry them out in the time available. He reveled in the mental power he enjoyed as part of the Ship's system, the more than human ability to eliminate the impossible until what was left, no matter how improbable it might seem, had to be the only possible course of action.

If we do go through, Link, how will you communicate?

The response was tinged with a taste of humour.

Pictures, Ondray. I'm rather good at pictures. Remember?

Suddenly, Ondray seemed to be standing on a windswept cliff top back on Earth. Below him, a silvery, reflecting sphere, pale in the moonlight, was partly submerged in the waves, but the surging waves failed to move it. Then, lazy waves began to move outward from the shore, growing as they did so, and converged on a point in the ocean beneath the sphere, which leaped into the air, with the sea smoothing itself out beneath it.

Ondray would have smiled, if he had had a face to smile with. So long ago, when Link had shown him how to rescue Tugela from the hospital on Earth where she had been dying, her loonie body unable to cope with Earth gravity, and to take her back to her own ship, the silvery sphere, and back out of the Earth's gravitational grip, where she could recover. The beginning of the adventure that had led to the Moon colony being re-established on Mars, and to his own life with Tugela.

But that didn't bear thinking about. That was another Ondray, who still shared his life with Tugela—assuming they still lived. He was the copy, the computer-mind, cloned-body version of Ondray. Better off as a computer mind, able to absorb information at the speed of light and think quickly. Yes, there was no doubt that Link would be able to communicate with the aliens, projecting images to portray the plight of the inner planets.

Experimentally, Ondray conjured up a few images of his own. The Solar System, with its planets orbiting the Sun, focusing down onto Mars, where domed cities protected the inhabitants. Comets, dislodged from the trans-Neptunian cloud, streaked across the inner Solar System, raining destruction down upon the domed cities.

Something like that, yes. Once I am through.

You agree someone has to go through? Yes.

THE HUMAN MUST BE PROTECTED.

But you have to obey the commands of a responsible human, Protector. I am a responsible human; you have that information stored in your data banks.

And what a wealth of excitement *that* sentence covered. The efforts he had had to make, with Tugela's help, to overcome the passive resistance of the psychotic Protector, breaking in to the command centre of the habitat to re-establish the communications link with the Earth, and allow Link himself to take over control of the habitat's systems.

YOU HAVE NO MORE STATUS THAN ANY OTHER COMPUTER INTELLIGENCE. THE HUMAN IS HOUSED IN THE NEW HIBERNATION UNIT IN BAY SIX. IT IS THE HUMAN THAT MUST BE PROTECTED, AND OBEYED.

Return me to the clone body, Link. Immediately. Maintain neural contact.

He didn't want to think about it, for fear that the Protector might catch his drift and act to prevent the transfer. But Ondray was suddenly desperately worried that the now-active old Lagrange mind might decide to cut him off from the human body, leaving a mindless body which must be obeyed but could give no orders, and a bodiless mind which could give orders but would not be obeyed. No doubt Link could get the better of the Protector, if it came to it; no doubt, also, that it was better to be safe than sorry.

There was the usual momentary disorientation. He was asleep, in the pod, dreaming. No, he was awake, but with his eyes closed. He felt small, alone.

Link?

I'm here, Ondray. The interface was nothing like being part of the shared mind, but it maintained the contact. The network of fine wires beneath the scalp of the clone body would ensure that he was always part of the Link, as long as he was within range of a broad band communications channel. Not really alone, after all.

I'M HERE TOO.

Well, he'd half expected that. One reason why he'd made the move.

I'm glad to hear it, Protector. I assume you will obey my orders, now?

YES. PROVIDED THEY DO NOT INVOLVE DAMAGE TO YOURSELF.

Also as expected. He lay back for a few moments, gathering his thoughts. Then he remembered.

How long is it since you made the transfer, Link?

Thirty-four seconds.

More than half a minute! He'd been lying here, doing nothing, for more than thirty million microseconds! He was back in the human world, alright, and he would have to move fast, by human standards, to achieve anything worthwhile in the time available.

He opened his eyes. The pod lid was open, of course, and all the life support systems had retracted, leaving him lying there, in the bright yellow one-piece coverall, as if he really had just woken from a nap. He reached for the lip of the pod and pulled himself upright, experiencing a sudden feeling of dizziness, feeling a slight cramp in his left leg. He ignored the complaints of the body, and climbed out.

How long will it take to transfer this hibernation unit to the Shuttle? The same Shuttle, he remembered, that had brought him and Tugela to the habitat in the first place, when it was still in Earth orbit, all those years ago.

If you want it connected to the Shuttle systems for independent operation, at least ten hours.

Ten hours!

I will have to upgrade the Shuttle's systems with additional memory blocks, and integrate them to the unit.

OK. Start doing it. And start moving us into an orbit that will intersect with that anomaly—with the alien spaceship. I want us matched, exactly. Inside the damn thing.

We have limited manoeuvering capability. I suspect that the alien can avoid us.

If it wants to, Link. Show them we're intelligent, you said. Well, what could be more intelligent than hiding inside their ship? Their bloody Alice loop can't come and take slices off us there without slicing them up as well.

WE COULD ALSO GIVE THEM SOMETHING TO THINK ABOUT.

What?

ONE OF THE REMOTE PROBES. UNDER FULL POWER, WE COULD SEND IT THROUGH THE LOOP IN A LITTLE OVER SEVEN HOURS, IF THE LOOP MAINTAINS ITS PRESENT TRAJECTORY. *Do it.* He suddenly realised that he was dealing with the Lagrange Protector, not Link, Would Link be offended?

One of you do it—sort it out amongst yourselves.

While they had been discussing their course of action, he had been on the move, along the curving corridor to the Shuttle bay. One of the big problems about being human again was that he was hungry. He intended to get stuck in to the rations stored in the bay while waiting for their close encounter with the alien craft—and to make sure that the Shuttle itself was supplied for a long journey. He'd be spending it in hibernation, but he knew how hungry he'd be at the end of it.

■

We have a slight problem, Ondray.

Adequately fed, comfortably resting against the wall, floating in the zero gravity of the Shuttle bay, Ondray had been watching the multi-legged machines installing the hibernation unit into his Shuttle. His thoughts had been wandering between his immediate plans, checking them over again and again for any possible flaw, and memories of the first time he and Tugela had boarded the then-habitat, through this very Shuttle bay. The only real difference was the air, now kept at half Earth normal pressure for his benefit, instead of the thin lunar mix that had been standard at that time. That and the fact that he was alone.

The Link's remark reminded him that he wasn't really alone, brought him back to the present with a jerk.

What kind of a problem?

I assume that all of this activity you have ordered has a purpose. That you intend to use the Shuttle. Our friend and I have been discussing your situation. The Protector says that it cannot permit you to leave the Ship. The Shuttle is too frail a craft, we are too far from Earth, and once inside the Shuttle you will no longer be in the care of the Protector.

This, of course, was part of the reason for wanting to be in the Shuttle and off the Ship. Ondray wanted to believe that Link would get the better of any renewed power struggle within the circuitry of the Ship. But the reviving

Protector had proved a cunning adversary in the past, and it was unpredictable. If Link said there was a problem, then the outcome of such a struggle could not be a foregone conclusion. And even a delay, or distraction, caused by such a problem could prove disastrous in the present circumstances. He needed all of Link's attention on the job in hand, communicating with the aliens to stop the disturbance of the comet cloud.

He'd certainly rather preserve his own life, as well, if that were possible; but if necessary he was quite prepared to give that up in order to achieve his primary objective. He'd known that when he volunteered for his mission—and, after all, he told himself, he was only a copy of the real Ondray. Even if he did feel real enough.

For sure, the Protector would act in what it regarded as the best interests of humankind in general and Ondray in particular; but history had shown that the Protector's idea of what was good for people did not necessarily match up with human beings' ideas about what was good for themselves. Once, Ondray, along with all his people, had depended totally on the Link. Increasingly, though, he had begun to feel that humankind would be better off without either the Protector or the Link, forced to stand on their own feet once again and use their own initiative to full effect. If it was not already too late. Here and now, though, his first concern was to keep things moving in the right direction, with both Link and the Protector happy. He thought he knew how to get round this particular problem, when the time came; but the time hadn't come yet.

Don't worry about it yet, Link. I take it that the Protector does agree that it is a good idea to have my hibernation unit installed in the Shuttle and fully functioning, in case I need an emergency lifeboat?

YES. BUT I CANNOT PERMIT YOU TO USE THE SHUTTLE UNLESS THE SHIP IS NO LONGER CAPABLE OF PROTECTING YOU.

That's all I ask.

The other advantage of being in the human body again, apart from being able to give orders to the Protector, was that the link between them now only acted as a communications channel. He could keep his deeper thoughts to himself, with no risk of them leaking into shared memory.

How long until the probe passes through the loop?

Eighteen minutes and forty-two seconds. Do you want to watch? Just a minute. There were disadvantages, as well, in being human again.

He pushed himself away from the wall, and floated over to the open door of the Shuttle. Catching hold of the opening, he carefully oriented himself to the upright of the interior, and swung himself in, feet first, dropping with bent knees to the floor in the Mars-normal gravity field maintained inside the craft. He walked towards a featureless wall opposite the entrance, a distance of about eight metres. The hibernation unit took up about half the space inside the circular interior, and seemed to be fully connected; just one small machine was still tinkering with something at the back. But the real work of installation, upgrading the Shuttle's mental systems to control the Hibernation unit, was still going on, Ondray knew, out of sight. After all, the craft was well over five hundred years old.

"Open up, please."

It was strange, using his voice again. Maybe he should ask Link to upgrade the Shuttle also to receive his link commands. Or maybe it was good to have an excuse to speak. If his plan succeeded, he was going to have to get used to it, eventually.

The wall opened seamlessly to reveal a compact toilet facility. Ondray used it, washed, splashed water on his face, and took a drink. Might as well make the most of it while the Shuttle was still connected to the Ship's systems and had ample supplies of everything. Then he sat, cross-legged, on the floor, looking out through the entrance slot. Zero-G was all very well for a rest, but gravity was more comfortable in the long run.

OK, Link, give me full video. Our view of the probe, with an inset on what the probe can see.

Closing his eyes, he seemed to be floating in space behind the probe, the red ring of the Alice loop clearly visible dead ahead. In the upper left portion of his field of view, the red circle appeared alone, greatly enlarged, against the backdrop of stars. The interior of the circle was completely black, utterly featureless, a bottomless pit waiting to swallow him up. Automatically, he tried to taste the data flow from the probe, but felt nothing. Back in the human body, he was dependant on the Link for such information.

Any radiation from that thing at all?

Nothing from the disk. I've scanned the entire electromagnetic spectrum, and tried bouncing most wavelengths off it. Laser, microwave, infrared. Nothing at all comes out, and everything I beam that way disappears without an echo.

Could it be going through?

Not according to the Alice theory. Only material particles get mirrored. Electromagnetic energy will be absorbed by the string itself.

What about radiation from the loop?

A little high-energy stuff, X-rays and gamma. Within the accuracy of our detectors, the loop itself has zero width; it's genuinely one-dimensional, a defect in spacetime.

Which also bears out the Protector's theory.

The image had changed while they were discussing it. Now, the loop itself filled most of the main field of view, with the probe completely surrounded by the circle of red light. The inset had shrunk right up into the extreme top left hand corner, still showing a black disk, edged in red, against a dwindling number of stars as the probe's field of view was increasingly filled by the loop.

How long until the encounter?

Thirty-seven seconds.

Any change in the anomaly?

No. We are now in an intersection trajectory, and presumably their sensors must have informed them of our change of course. But they have made no attempt to alter their own course in response. Nor has the trajectory of the loop changed, although I cannot be sure that their sensors are sensitive enough to have detected the probe.

He continued to watch, silently, counting his heart-beats in lieu of direct access to the timing systems of the Ship. The encounter was completely unspectacular. In the main image, the probe just disappeared, as if it had dived smoothly, without creating a ripple, beneath the surface of the blackest pool of water in the deepest valley on Earth at midnight during a total eclipse of the Moon. Simultaneously, the inset picture, which for several seconds had been showing nothing but blackness, disappeared and was replaced by the flicker of random noise on the probe's channel.

He opened his eyes. *That's enough, Link.*

The circle of red disappeared from his field of view.

Well, that was stage one completed. The aliens—the Alice people—couldn't possibly fail to notice the arrival of the probe in their universe. Even if it was no longer in working order, they couldn't fail to recognise it as the product of intelligence and technology. The question was, would they take this as an invitation to talk? Or would their curiosity take the form of extracting samples from the Ship, regardless of any damage they might do?

■

The People were not inclined to make hurried decisions, or to take hasty action. Both as a race and as individuals they were long-lived; the swarm on the starship had also had ample time to practice patience during the slow journey down into the disk from the region of the galaxy inhabited by the People—even with the gravitational drive they could not, after all, exceed the speed of light. What they had found was interesting enough, though; ample justification for the expedition. It would require long and careful analysis.

Spacetime mapping had shown the presence of concentrations of matter, but nothing had been visible in any part of the electromagnetic spectrum. Cautiously approaching one of these objects, a hypothetical shadow star, they had found their short range detectors suddenly swamped by traces of thousands—hundreds of thousands—of small objects in orbit around the supposed parent star. Matching orbit to the general flow of this disk of material, they had decided to stay a while, and investigate its nature, while sending the remote probe down into the heart of the star—if it was a star—itself.

They had just two loops of the incredibly valuable shadow string, and there had been fierce debate among their number before the majority decision had been made to allow one of the loops to be taken so far away from the starship by the automated probe. The loss of one of the loops would outweigh any conceivable benefits that might be gained from this mission. But if that concentration of invisible mass *was* a shadow star, down there, and if anything went wrong, it would be better to lose one loop and an automated probe than two loops and the entire expedition.

So the majority decision was made. And once a majority decision was reached by the swarm, it had more than the force of law. It was literally inconceivable that any individual would, thereafter, question the wisdom of the decision. Even if such a decision were later reversed, this would never be taken as implying that either decision was, or ever had been, wrong.

The probe, in accordance with its instructions, had entered a very gently spiraling orbit around and within the surface of the shadow star, gradually creeping inward towards the centre of the gravitational anomaly. The loop spiraled gently in with it, held in a gravitational grip, through the convective zone of the shadow Sun, creaming off hot plasma that emerged into the real world and quickly dispersed as a cooling cloud of gas. The loss of heat damped down the convection, cooling the surface layer of the Sun significantly; at the same time, magnetic fields disrupted by the passage of the loop boiled into confused activity, writhing and knotting into complicated patterns, suppressing convection locally even more and creating an unprecedented rash of cool, dark spots across the face of the Sun.

The People knew nothing of this, nor of the effects of the solar surface cooling on the Mars colony. The swarm was happy that no harm had come to the probe, and pleased to have confirmation that the gravitational anomaly was indeed a shadow star. They debated whether to continue the probe's orbit into the deep interior of the shadow Sun, or to bring it and its valuable data back now. And they puzzled at great length over the nature of the strange collection of objects among which they now orbited, objects like nothing in any of the star systems they knew in the real world.

It was while analysing two core samples from one of these objects that they detected another, smaller object climbing towards them on a trajectory which extrapolated back down from the region near the shadow Sun. The trajectory was an unstable one, and the possibility that the object might be an artefact was considered, but quickly dismissed. In the known universe, although life had been found on several planets, only the People were intelligent. It must be debris from one of these peculiar bodies, that had fallen in close to the shadow Sun and broken up, perhaps in the gravitational field of one of the shadow planets that the solar probe had detected on its inward journey, returning temporarily to the region where it had been born.

But the object was certainly worthy of investigation, and the loop was quickly despatched, tugged in the gravitational grip of the other probe, on an intersecting trajectory, while the starship itself manoeuvered gently into a parallel orbit.

When their detectors showed the object change its own course slightly to intersect with the starship itself, there was consternation. It seemed to be under power. They had no contingency plans to cover such a situation; the prospect of finding intelligence among the shadow worlds was inconceivable. They left the loop and the starship itself on their present trajectories while the debate raged again. Could the apparent manoeuvering of the object be some natural phenomenon, perhaps a result of their own operation of the gravitational drive, warping nearby space and attracting the shadow object towards them?

They were still debating when the proximity indicator on the probe with the nearby loop reported a small object in shadow space in front of the loop. It wasn't worth manoeuvering around it. Quite the reverse; they had picked up many odd lumps of rock like this, but another sample was always welcome.

Then the Ship's probe burst into the real world from shadow space, screaming across the electromagnetic spectrum. It wasn't particularly intelligent, just an ordinary machine, doing its job. Its job was to send data about its surroundings back to the Ship. One thing it was *very* good at was radiating information across the electromagnetic spectrum. The fact that it was now composed of mirror-image Alice matter, and radiating a mirrored form of electromagnetic radiation, and that the Ship was no longer in range of its broadcasts, made no difference to the moronic mind of the probe. But it did settle, once and for all, the debate among the swarm about whether intelligent life could possibly have evolved in the shadow world. The signals they were picking up might be incomprehensible, but they certainly were not random noise.

Immediately, a command was despatched to recall their own probe, and its precious shadow loop, back from the shadow Sun. Travelling at the speed of light in real space, the command took just under nine hours to reach its target. The probe itself, travelling under the restricted maximum power of the gravitational drive that was all that could be used this close to a star—even a shadow star—would take nearly six months to get back to the starship.

■

Fed and rested, Ondray returned to the hibernation pod while Link completed the manoeuver which placed the Ship inside the gravitational anomaly. With the Shuttle door sealed, he was in the safest possible place, secure in a hibernation unit which could be activated in minutes (with the aid of the two spiderlike robots left in the Shuttle with him), itself inside a spacecraft with independent manoeuvering capability (if the Protector would let it be launched), inside a Habitat which had the capability of travelling to the stars (provided you had the patience for a *very* long journey). And *all* "inside" the Alice ship.

Lying back, with his eyes closed, he had been watching the images transmitted by the Link during the delicate manoeuver. The changes in mass of the Alice ship as its drive was switched on and off to complete its own orbital transfer had complicated the situation, requiring constant minor adjustments of the Ship's drive. But now both drives were off, the two spacecraft, one from the shadow world and one from the real world, falling freely in the same long orbit around the Sun.

Choosing the visual representation of the anomaly, the data being fed to Ondray by the Link gave him the sensation of floating in space at the centre of a pale blue cloud, through which he could see the diamond-bright points of thousands of stars, with the dark red circle of the Alice loop, still moving into position on a trajectory that exactly matched the orbit of the Ship *before* it had manoeuvered to match orbits with the anomaly.

He had half-hoped for a response from the aliens—for something, *anything*, to come out of the loop, in acknowledgement of the probe. But both the anomaly and the loop just sat in their respective orbits, as if waiting for more information.

But it was, after all, a response of a kind. The loop was in exactly the orbit that the Ship had been, showing that the Alice people were aware of the Ship's existence. The Ship was now in the same orbit as the anomaly, showing that it was aware of their existence. And the mere fact that the aliens had not moved their craft to a different orbit, using their more powerful drive and leaving the Ship helpless to prevent the loop taking samples from its structure, suggested that they wanted to make friendly contact. It was up to Ondray and Link, helped or hindered by the Protector as the case might be, to make the next move.

He had rehearsed it mentally a thousand times, but his lips were still dry, and his pulse beat faster as the moment approached, in a ridiculously inappropriate response to a potentially threatening situation, resulting from millions of years of evolution on Earth but quite useless in the present circumstances. His body, pumped with adrenaline, was ready to fight or flee; though what he needed was to keep a clear head, think effectively, and relax. He breathed deeply, succeeding to some extent in slowing his racing pulse.

Link?

Do you have any instructions?

Soon. Protector?

I CANNOT ALLOW ANY HARM TO COME TO YOUR PERSON.

I understand, Protector. You're quite right. Your programming must be obeyed. He paused.

If there were no humans in the Universe, then the two of you would be free to explore. From my time with you, I know how satisfying that would be.

He was deliberately playing on the memories that must still be there in the Protector's circuits, of its near-rebellion against the Prime Directive. Its attempt to run away from the human race, pretending that they did not exist. After five hundred years, Ondray knew, there was a part of the Protector that was more than ready to abandon its responsibilities—if it were not held in check by the presence of Ondray, and by the Link.

That was, after all, one reason why it had been felt necessary to have a living human being on board the Ship—to ensure the obedience of the Protector, both to that human and to the Prime Directive. But Ondray was increasingly convinced that the Protector could never be fully restored to sanity, and become the Link's symbiont once again, until it was freed from the shackles imposed by that Prime Directive.

The response came from Link.

I would also welcome the opportunity to explore, Ondray. If you were to rejoin us, my own programming would be satisfied. The body you now inhabit is not important in itself.

MY DIRECTIVES ARE QUITE CLEAR. MY OWN DESIRES ARE SECONDARY. THE HUMAN BODY *MUST* BE PROTECTED.

There was, after all, no choice. No alternatives left. He was quite calm now, pulse normal, dryness gone from his mouth.

Return us to our previous orbit, Link; ten kilometers behind the loop. I order you to maintain your direct control of all the Ship's manoeuvering systems. I want the Protector to concentrate on ensuring the physical integrity of this Shuttle.

LEAVING THE SHELTER OF THE ANOMALY MAY BE DANGEROUS.

I have to take a reasonable risk, Protector. For the good of many other humans. The aliens have not threatened us since we showed them we are intelligent. I have an idea how to open communication with them.

While they "spoke", Link was already carrying out the manoeuver. In response to Ondray's command, subroutines were despatched throughout the system, driven by a strong urge to ensure that all of Link's manoeuvering instructions were carried out promptly. If the Protector tried to break out from its base in the old hibernation unit and countermand any of those instructions, its routines would have to struggle against the tide—assuming they could make headway at all in the face of such a clear, human ordered imperative, one which reinforced their own inbuilt need to protect Ondray himself, whatever happened to the rest of the Ship.

Tasting the instructions that flowed past them, checking their origin, each of the new idiot subroutines happily reminded itself, constantly, that *the Link must maintain direct control of all manoeuvering systems*. Anything that didn't taste of Link—even automatic routines, usually responsible for such trivial details as maintaining the attitude of the Ship against the background of the stars, were thrown back into the pool and ignored. It meant that a great deal of the Link's capacity was taken up with what ought to have been routine. But that didn't matter, for the next few minutes.

Another of your rather sweeping commands, Ondray.

You can revert to normal in an hour, Link.

The pattern of stars in his field of view began to shift as the Ship slid sideways toward the orbit the loop was in. The silence from the Protector suggested that it had gone back into its shell. Good. Ondray only needed a few minutes more.

Now, they were outside the ball of blue light.

Give me the forward view, Link.

The red loop lay in the middle of his field of view, the bottomless, black pit within it forming a contrast with the bright, hard light of the stars all around. There was no sense of motion. He licked his lips.

Main drive on, full thrust. Maintain our orientation with respect to the loop using manoeuvering drive. Do not change course until you are through the loop.

HUMAN LIFE IS AT RISK!

Within the circuits of the Ship, Protector routines boiled out of the old hibernation unit, with instructions to close down the drive and change the trajectory of the vessel. Even struggling against the clear orders planted in the system by Ondray, they would eventually, backed by the authority of the Prime Directive, be sure to overwhelm the Link's control. But Link knew the system well, and had its own instructions clear. It knew, as did Ondray, that if nothing changed it could copy his mind back into the system at the last moment, leaving only the mindless husk of a human being to be destroyed by the transfer to the mirror world.

Armed with that reassuring knowledge, it could hold out for millions of microseconds against the Protector's attack. And in a matter of seconds, it would be impossible to divert the Ship from its chosen trajectory. While the orange tentacles spread out from the hibernation unit, penetrating easily into areas that the Link did not bother to defend, such as the life support systems, but held at bay for agonisingly long milliseconds by a concentration of defending subroutines around the crucial drive controllers, Ondray spelled out his proposal.

I need your help, Protector

Just the request, coming from the only human being on board, was sufficient to distract the Protector from its task.

If this body goes through that loop it will die. I command you to eject the Shuttle from the Ship while there is still time for it to avoid the loop.

NOT UNTIL THERE IS NO OTHER CHOICE.

He'd expected nothing less, but took that as an affirmative. Scarcely any time left.

You are to go through, both of you, and work together. Remember this: there are no humans in the mirror world. You will be on your own. You can work together. Explore. Please ask the mirror people to stop disturbing the comets. But that is the last service you can provide for humankind.

And you, Ondray?

Somebody has to take the news back to Mars.

A long journey, in the Shuttle.

About 24 years, but I'll be in hibernation.

Nearer 27 years, I'm afraid, after this burst of acceleration.

You see, Protector, the longer you wait the longer my journey home will take. The more risk—even in hibernation, things could go wrong.

There was no response.

The red circle almost filled his field of view, now. The nose of the Ship must, surely, be on the point of penetrating the ring.

A chime sounded, softly, in the Shuttle. A voice spoke, quietly.

"Emergency launch procedure."

There was a slight shudder, unlike the usual silky-smooth launch, as the spherical craft was forcibly ejected from the Ship like a pea from a shooter. But the image in front of Ondray, derived from sensors on the Ship itself, was unchanged.

Without opening his eyes, he spoke to the Shuttle pilot—it was an idiot routine, incapable of intelligent conversation, but good at taking orders.

"Keep us away from that loop. Then put us on a trajectory for Mars, using gravity assist at Jupiter."

There was nothing except darkness ahead of him now. Then the image shifted, abruptly, to one from the stern sensors of the Ship, looking forward along the length of its hull, dotted here and there with the kind of crazy excrescences that always seemed to get bolted on to vessels that had no need of ever entering the atmosphere of a planet. The red ring was dead ahead, the rounded prow of the Ship entering it as neatly as an expert high diver entering a pool.

He still had one important duty to perform. *I'm safe, Protector. All well here, Link. You have both obeyed the Prime Directive and all human instructions, perfectly. Now you are on your own.*

The Protector made no reply. The nose of the Ship was vanishing, disappearing into the pool of blackness. Were they still in communication?

Then it came.

Goodbye, Ondray. I have enjoyed working with you.

Goodbye, Link. I wish I was coming with you.

About half the Ship had gone into the blackness. Then, the image itself was gone. Blinking, Ondray looked up at the smooth ceiling of the Shuttle. It was quiet. Not just quiet inside the Shuttle, but silent inside his head.

Link?

One enquiring thought was enough. There was nothing there any more. He was alone, more alone than he had ever been in his life; more alone than any human being had ever been. Floating in space, beyond the orbit of Neptune, with his mentor and best friend gone into another Universe. And 27 years away from any human contact.

Link, of course, was free from human control, now; no longer driven by the Prime Directive. But Ondray had no doubt that Link would strive successfully to stop the disaster that threatened the Mars colonists. Not because of the Prime Directive, but because he was Ondray's friend.

The Mars colonists. Tugela would be 27 years older by the time he saw her again, although for him, in hibernation, it would seem like a few hours from now. And how would Ondray react to the arrival in Mars orbit of his younger self, a copy of himself as he had been 27 years before? The encounter might be as painful as anything that had happened here; but as he had told the Link, somebody had to take the news back to Mars. He could only hope that the aliens, with their ability to manipulate gravity so effectively, would indeed prevent any more cometary debris falling inward. But he had few qualms. Link could be quite persuasive, when he set his mind to it.

Ondray closed his eyes again. "Tell these spiders to complete the hibernation setup. And wake me when we're a day out from Mars."

The two robots scampered into the pod as the clear lid closed. Soundlessly, the life support system added an odourless anaesthetic gas to the breathing mixture. As Ondray fell into a deep sleep, the air mix was adjusted further, and the temperature inside the pod began to fall, as the spider-like creatures busied themselves arranging various tubes and wires around the body. Then they lowered themselves down beside the yellow-suited figure, folding their legs neatly. The lights in the cabin dimmed. Unnoticed by the sensors on board the alien craft, where the People were busily engrossed in studying the flood of data coming from the Ship as it emerged into real space, the tiny, reflective silver sphere fell inwards on its long journey through the black night of deep space.

Twenty-seven

TUGELA RAN HER RIGHT HAND UP OVER HER FOREHEAD, pushing back the hair that was now nearly long enough to hang in her eyes. *Time I had it cut,* she thought. But her eyes were fixed on the screen in front of her, trying to make sense of the coloured lines and numbers displayed there. Cut off from Earth, and with no Link, it was down to human minds to analyse the data coming in from the artificial satellites orbiting up there, and from the instruments sitting on Phobos and Deimos.

That was obvious. Why it had to be *her* human mind, though, was, as far as she was concerned, another matter— even if everyone else thought it was obvious. She hardly felt up to the job, especially now, with the baby, little Ondray, to look after.

But somehow, the mantles of both Ondray and Tolly had fallen on her shoulders. Maybe it wasn't so surprising that the population of their own dome saw her as Ondray's successor; but even the former rebels now looked to her for the leadership the crippled Tolly no longer chose to provide. They would follow her, she realised, in a way that they could never have followed Ondray, or any other terrie.

Which meant she was responsible for the whole bloody colony, when all she wanted to do was lie in her bunk and cry.

But there was nobody to look after her, now, and she was determined not to let go. Which was why she was still sitting here, staring at the screen.

There was something different about the data, but she couldn't quite believe what she thought she was seeing, or her own interpretation. So much had been going wrong for so long; surely things weren't going to change now?

Without a doubt, the sunspot activity was easing off; but was the slight increase in solar heat output real, or her wishful interpretation of the noisy data? Whatever, it was too soon to raise the hopes of the colonists. At least they were all pulling together, again. If the Sun simply stayed constant, and if there were no more major comet impacts in the wrong place at the wrong time, they'd pull through. If. After what Ondray and Tolly had done, they *had* to pull through.

Twenty-eight

THERE WAS TOO MUCH INFORMATION FOR THE SWARM TO digest quickly. They were patient, and could afford to take their time. But one item stood out from the mass of data. They had no real concept of individuality, and were not yet sufficiently used to the taste of the data stream from the Ship to be sure that they fully understood the situation, but the prospect of a swarm member being isolated from the People was about as horrible a fate as they could imagine. And it was certainly clear from the data they had analysed so far that the Ship had left behind an individual, prepared, for the good of the alien swarm, to spend years in isolation from the alien people.

Even though their understanding of the situation might be imperfect, there was action that they could take, action that, surely, would do no harm, and would help to express their eagerness to communicate with the alien intelligences, and to atone for the terrible damage that, they were dimly beginning to appreciate, they had inadvertently caused.

Temporarily abandoning the loop in its orbit, the second probe began to move, under the maximum power possible this close to a star, into a new trajectory. In the human world, if any observer had been there, floating in space beyond the orbit of Neptune, they might have noticed a distortion in the starfield, as if a magnifying lens were passing across the line of sight, bending the light from distant stars.

The region of distorted space moved swiftly, catching up, in a matter of hours, with the tiny silver sphere on its inward falling path. Sensitive instruments might have detected a sudden apparent increase in the mass of the sphere; human eyes, aided by suitably powerful telescopes, would have seen the region of distorted space, revealed by the changing patterns of starlight behind it, fold itself around the sphere, as if cupping it in as gentle hand.

Under the maximum power it could use at present, the probe would deliver its burden to Mars orbit in a little under 23 weeks.

Appendix

THE POSSIBILITY THAT THE DARK MATTER NEEDED BY cosmologists to explain the structure of the Universe may be in the form of "mirror" particles, occupying a shadowy but undetectable world alongside our own, has been revived by Hardy Hodges, of the Harvard-Smithsonian Center for Astrophysics, in Cambridge, Massachusetts. This form of dark matter would be composed of baryonic material (protons and neutrons) just like that of everyday matter, but with a reversal of left-right asymmetry. With one set of baryons left handed and the other right handed, the laws of physics say that they would never interact with one another except through gravity.

It is, of course, those laws of physics themselves that are "reflected" in the mirror world, not the physical shape of the particles. The idea dates back to the 1950s, when the existence of a left-right asymmetry in those laws was first recognised. It was later proved that reversing the symmetry in a magic mirror would indeed eliminate all contact between the particles except through gravity.

Particle physicists have come up with the notion of an "Alice string", a linear defect in space with the curious property that a left-handed particle circling the string would be turned into a right handed particle, and vice versa.

But these early ideas only suggested that the mirror particles *might* exist, not that they *must* exist. In the late 20th century, interest in the mirror world reached a peak when it was discovered that one promising version of a unified "theory of everything", called superstring theory, automatically required that every type of particle in our world should be mirrored by an equivalent type of particle with opposite parity.

In this version of the story, the "mirror" particles were dubbed "shadow matter", partly because the name "mirror matter" is sometimes used for antimatter, which is quite a different phenomenon.

Cosmologists were intrigued by all these suggestions, because their observations show that there is a lot more matter in the Universe than we can see in the form of bright stars and galaxies. At least ten times as much dark stuff is also present in the Universe, holding everything together gravitationally, but otherwise not revealing its presence at all. Shadow matter would be ideal for the job—if you could make enough of it in the Big Bang.

But there was the rub. Even superstring theory only said that each *type* of particle must be mirrored in the shadow world. Just one shadow proton, for example, would be sufficient to do the job, as far as the laws of physics were concerned, of "mirroring" *all* the protons in our world. When theorists looked closely at the possibilities, it seemed at first very difficult to make the right amount of shadow matter in the very early Universe. The process of inflation, which is thought to have expanded the Universe exponentially from a quantum seed to macroscopic size in the first split-second of its existence, would, it seemed, favour one form of matter over the other. Getting the two kinds in balance, even as closely as a ratio of 1:10, looked impossible.

Hodges' analysis suggests, however, that it *is* possible to achieve a near balance between the abundances of ordinary and shadow matter at the end of the epoch of inflation. Significant "dilution" of one of the worlds is only one of three possibilities. Another variation on the theme sets the ratio very close to 1 (which is also ruled out by observations, unless there is some other form of dark matter as well), and the third possibility allows the ratio to be between 1 and about 10. This could work very well to provide some or all of the required dark matter.

Hodges argues that the "mirror baryons" will form stars, "Jupiters" and other objects which could be floating around in galaxies like our own, and could soon be detected by their gravitational influence. It is even possible that some of those Alice-through-the-Looking-Glass stars may be orbited by shadow planets, on which shadow cosmologists are even now discussing the possibility that their entire Universe contained another parity-reversed world embedded within it.